The Real People
Book Seven

THE WAR TRAIL NORTH

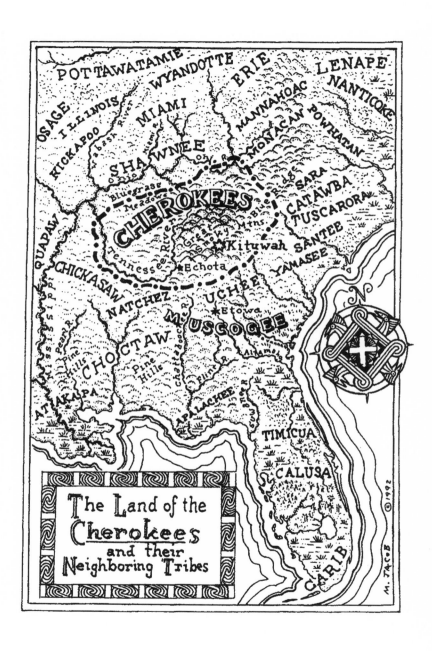

The Land of the Cherokees and their Neighboring Tribes

ROBERT J. CONLEY

The War
Trail North

UNIVERSITY OF OKLAHOMA PRESS

Norman

With the exception of historical figures, all of the characters in this book are fictitious, and any resemblance to actual persons, living or dead, is purely coincidental.

Library of Congress Cataloging-in-Publication Data

Conley, Robert J.
    The war trail north / Robert J. Conley — Oklahoma paperbacks ed.
      p. cm.
    ISBN 0-8061-3278-7 (alk. paper)
    1. Cherokee Indians—Fiction. 2. Seneca Indians—Fiction. I. Title.

PS3553.O494 W28 2000
813'.54—dc21

                              00-037403

The paper in this book meets the guidelines for permanence and durability of the Committee on Production Guidelines for Book Longevity of the Council on Library Resources, Inc. ∞

Oklahoma Paperbacks edition published by the University of Oklahoma Press, Norman, Publishing Division of the University. Manufactured in the U.S.A. First edition, 1995. First printing of the University of Oklahoma Press edition, 2000.

1 2 3 4 5 6 7 8 9 10

THE WAR TRAIL NORTH

One

HIADEONI, of *Nun-da-wa-oh-noh*, the People of the Great Hill, was deep in enemy country. He was on a mission. His mother's brother, the man who had always been closest to him, who had taught him all the ways of the hunt and of war, who had disciplined him when he had been an unruly child and a rebellious young man, Gana, the great man, had been killed by warriors of the *Oyada'ge'onnon*, the Cave People. He had sworn that he would balance things out for his lost uncle. He would kill at least one of these Cave People, and he would do so on this trip. When he had left his home some days before, he had told the entire population of his town that he would not return until he had accomplished his sworn and sacred mission.

Hiadeoni knew that he was nearing a town. The road below him was well traveled, and he had ventured down a time or two to examine the signs on the road. He had seen the footprints of several people traveling in both directions. He also had noticed that the game was not quite so plentiful as it had been before. He knew that a town was near.

He climbed high up the mountainside in order to give himself the widest possible view of his surroundings. Down below he could not see very far, for the mountains rose to his left, and on the other side of the road the river ran. Both the mountainside and the opposite bank of the river were thick with lush, dark forest.

But up on the ridge he commanded a good view of the road below for quite some distance, and he figured that he would also be able to keep the town in view before he was too close for comfort.

His plan was not well formed, but the general practice he intended to follow was common. He would locate the town and take some time, perhaps as much as several days, to look it over. He would be watching for one of two things: a lone traveler coming out or going into the town, perhaps a lone hunter; or a house built out away from the town where a family lived in some isolation.

It would, of course, be utterly foolish to attempt anything else. It would be more than foolish. It would be crazy for a single avenger to go into a populous town. He was not suicidal, and he fully intended to return home to his own land in triumph. He would have to catch one of the Cave People alone.

Making his lonely way toward his goal, Hiadeoni recalled tales of the great warriors of his people, the People of the Great Hill, and the tales gave him the strength and determination to continue. After this adventure was over, he thought, he too would become the hero of a tale often told in the longhouses of the *Ong-weh-oh-weh*, the People of the Extended Lodge.

Then at last he saw the town. The road below led right up to its only entrance. He estimated it was a town of maybe 250 people, surrounded by a stockade fence with overlapping parallel ends which formed a narrow passageway into the town. In a fortified place such as this, he thought, the warriors would be constantly on the lookout for attack.

He felt his heart pound inside his chest. His mission had suddenly become more dangerous, and therefore his ultimate success would be even more praiseworthy. He was glad to have discovered such a town.

He recalled that the mountain passes into the country of the Cave People were well guarded, and he was proud of the way in which he had managed to avoid detection. By working his way around and behind the guards, not only had he gotten himself into the heart of their country, but very close to one of their fortress towns. But from here on, he knew, he would have to be especially watchful. He would have to try to make himself invisible to the eyes of his enemies.

Young Puppy had gone hunting. It was a special hunt for him, one which involved a special challenge, for it was his first hunt alone. His older brother, Awi-ekwa, Big Deer, had also gone out alone. On this day, of all days, Young Puppy wanted badly to be the one to bring back the first deer to present to their mother. He wanted to show them all that he was as good a hunter as his brother, and that he was as good a man as any in his town of Stikoyi. This was the first real challenge to his manhood, and he was desperate to meet it with success.

He had left home early in the morning, just as the sun was beginning her climb up the underside of the great Sky Vault, crawling toward her daughter's house directly overhead. Already the sun was halfway there, and Young Puppy was a good distance away from Stikoyi. He was beginning to feel that it would not be much longer. Soon, he thought, he would see *awi*, the deer.

Awi-ekwa, Big Deer, also hunted out from Stikoyi, but he had not gone as far out as his younger brother. He was proud of Young Puppy, and he wanted to see him become a successful and respected hunter. However, there was a matter of pride as well as his own reputation to consider. He did not want to be bested by his younger brother. It would be well enough, he thought, for Young Puppy to bring something home, but it should not be a better kill than his own, nor should Young Puppy return home first.

Therefore Awi-ekwa had not gone as far away from Stikoyi as he might have otherwise. It was true that the game was less plentiful near the town, but he had confidence in his own abilities, and he was sure that if any deer or big deer were to be found anywhere near the town, he would find it. When he had gone a ways down the road from Stikoyi, he started to climb the tree-covered mountain on the south side of the road. He was certain, that up there somewhere, he would find what he was looking for.

Awi-ekwa reached the top of the mountain. Soon he saw the neighboring town of Kituwah down below, and only then did he realize that he had gone so far. He was very close to where *Ani-wahya*, the Wolf People, would be guarding the mountain pass to keep any potential intruders out of the land of *Ani-yunwi-ya*, the Real People. He stopped to think for a moment, and to catch his breath after the long climb.

He would be unlikely to locate any animals near where the guards kept watch. He knew that. On the other hand, he did not want to be caught sneaking around too close to them either. If he surprised them, he might be mistaken for an intruder. He decided that he would approach them and identify himself. Then they would know that one of the Real People was hunting in the vicinity, and they would not mistake him for anyone else.

He walked on toward the spot where he knew the Wolves would be watching. Soon he was there, or at least, he was very close. He thought that he should be able to see them just up ahead, but he could not. He stopped and stood very still. Then it occurred to him that they had seen him, that they were there just ahead, hidden in the brush in order to see who was approaching.

"*'Siyo, Ani-wahya,*" he called.

He waited, but there was no immediate response to his greeting to the Wolf People. He looked around, still standing in the same spot.

"*Ayuh* Awi-ekwa," he called out to identify himself, "of the Long Hair People. I live in Stikoyi. Are you there?"

A man stepped out from behind a tree and held a hand up in greeting. Awi-ekwa walked toward him.

"I'm hunting," he said, "and when I realized that I was so close to the place where you watch, I thought that I should let you know."

Two other Wolves appeared, and the three of them approached Awi-ekwa. He recognized two of them as Trotting Wolf and He-Kills-Quickly. He did not know the third, but he did see that all three men were heavily armed.

" 'Siyo, Trotting Wolf," he said. "It's good to see you, my friend. And you, He-Kills-Quickly. I don't know this other one here."

"This is Asquani," said Trotting Wolf.

" 'Siyo, Asquani," said Awi-ekwa. He had heard of the young man who was the son of a Timucua woman and a white man, one of the men they called *Ani-Asquani*. He had also heard that this young man known as Asquani had been adopted by the Wolf People.

"*Osiyo*," said 'Squani.

"It's good to see you too, Awi-ekwa," said Trotting Wolf, "but I don't think you'll find anything to hunt around here."

"No, I don't think so either," said Awi-ekwa. "Maybe back that way a little. I was just so close to you that I came over here to let you know. That's all."

"It's good that you did," said He-Kills-Quickly. "If we had heard you moving around back there, we might have come to see who it was."

"Yes. That's what I thought too. So is everything quiet around here?"

"Yes. No one has been by this way for several days now, but that's the way we want it," said Trotting Wolf. "We sure don't want any of those ugly, hairy-faced white people coming into our country."

"Or anyone who might be their friends or allies," said 'Squani. "We can trust no one these days. No one but ourselves."

"That's true," said Awi-ekwa. "The stories we've heard

about the white men are terrible. And now there are two different tribes of them, they say."

"Maybe more," said Trotting Wolf. "At least three, I think. I've heard about three."

"But some of them are not as bad as others," said Asquani.

"Yes," said Trotting Wolf. "That's true." He remembered the time not so long ago when he had gone with Asquani to drive the *Ani-Asquani*, for whom the young man had been named, from their settlement on the Dark Island. Some white men from a different tribe had helped them.

"Well, anyhow," said Awi-ekwa, "I'm glad that you're here, you Wolves. I feel safer in my home, and even out like this for a hunt. So now that you know I'm around, I'll go on."

Awi-ekwa turned and started to walk away from the Wolves, but the voice of Trotting Wolf stopped him for just a moment.

"When you've made your kill," he called out, "come again to see us. We could use some fresh meat up here."

The three Wolves laughed, and Awi-ekwa gave them a broad smile.

"I will," he said. "We'll have a good meal here together before I go back to my home."

Far to the other side of Stikoyi, deep in the woods, Young Puppy had been following a stream. Somewhere along the way, he expected to find a deer that had come down for a drink of cool water, but so far he had not come across one.

He knew, though, that he had worked his way close to a browsing field, a place in the forest which had been cleared by the Real People in order to attract grazing animals. They had girdled the trees and let them die, then set a fire to clear the land and allow new grass to grow. Eventually the grass had grown tall, attracting deer and big deer, and even an occasional buffalo wandered in there to graze.

He decided to make his way over to the field. He climbed up a slight incline to move away from the stream. The area was rocky and thick with lush green growth. Even after the ground beneath his feet had leveled off, the forest was still thick. The canopy of leafy branches overhead refused admittance even to the powerful light of the sun.

When he reached the edge of the field, he was still within the darkness of the forest, but looking out into the bright open clearing. And there he saw it. His heart leapt with joy and excitement. It was a big deer, *awi-ekwa*, the name animal of his own older brother. How wonderful it would be to bring home such a kill.

He moved through the woods, keeping himself in the dark shadows, circling the field to find the best place for a good shot at the big deer. He moved slowly and carefully. He did not want the big deer to hear him or detect any movement from him. The big deer seemed to be totally unaware of his presence, completely oblivious to any possible danger.

At last Young Puppy stopped beside a large oak tree. He would not be able to get any closer, and there was nothing but tall grass between him and the big deer. He found that he was holding his breath, so he slowly took in a deep lungful of air. Carefully, quietly, slowly, he removed an arrow from his quiver. He looked at it. It was a good straight one, well tipped and well fletched.

He nocked it, took careful aim and pulled back the string to the side of his face. Holding his position for a moment, he said a brief prayer for the flight of the arrow, and then he let it go.

The vibrating string sang, and the arrow hit its mark with a thud. It sank deep. The big deer bleated and leapt forward. It stopped and sank to its knees, struggled to rise again and then fell over on its side. Young Puppy pulled the knife at his waist out of the sheath and ran toward the big deer.

Almost upon it, he approached the animal cautiously, for the big deer could still be dangerous if it was not dead. It did not move, however. Still, he cut its throat to be sure and to let it bleed. Then he knelt beside it and offered up an apology and an explanation to the spirit of the big deer.

That done, he set to work preparing the carcass to be carried back home across his shoulders to Stikoyi. It would be a long and tiring trip, he told himself, for this would be a heavy load. But his spirits were not dampened even by that forbidding prospect. His first hunt alone had been a great success. He was anxious to walk into Stikoyi, down the streets to his mother's house, with this particular burden on his back.

Two

HIADEONI had seen the two men leave the town. Even from the distance of his safe hiding place high on the hill, he could tell that one was younger than the other. The young one was probably inexperienced, and would be easier to kill, but the older one would present more of a challenge and therefore would bring him more honor. While he was considering these things, the younger one moved off alone toward the river, in a direction away from where Hiadeoni waited. The other one moved toward the very hillside on which he sat. The decision was made for him. He would watch the older one and await his chance.

Hiadeoni did not want to attack the man too close to the town for fear of alerting others to his presence, so he decided to watch and track him for a time. He would let the man get well away from his home. He would watch and wait for the perfect opportunity, and then he would strike.

As the man climbed the hill, Hiadeoni lost sight of him.

He knew that the hunter was moving in his direction, though, so he was not worried. The hillside was thick with trees and brush. The man would have to keep to the pathway. Hiadeoni moved back off the path and waited quietly. Soon he saw the man again. He stayed hidden and let him pass by.

Hiadeoni had been on the mountain top long enough to know that just behind him on the ridge was the beginning of a gradual rise to a ledge which eventually hovered above the path. If the hunter kept to the path, and Hiadeoni took to the ridge, he would find himself up above his prey. He moved to the ridge, taking care to keep as quiet as possible. He was not in a hurry.

Again he lost sight of the hunter, but he was not worried. The man was obviously following the path, so Hiadeoni knew that he would find him again. Although he had not yet investigated the high ledge above the path, he had seen it from a distance, and knew that from up there he would be able to relocate the Cave Person easily once he reached the summit. He kept moving at an easy and careful pace.

He was almost there when he heard the voices, and he was startled. He had allowed the hunter to get far enough away from the town in order to avoid alerting others only to unexpectedly encounter someone on the path below the ledge. He saw an outcropping of rocks just on the rim, and he moved to it with his heart pounding loudly in his chest, wondering just what he had stumbled into. The voices from below were clearer and more distinct. He breathed slowly and deeply, straining to hear, as he carefully peered over the rocks.

Down below on the path he could see the hunter he had

been following talking with three other warriors. What kind of a meeting was this? He knew that he could not fight four of them, and he was beginning to think that he had made a mistake in not following the young hunter. Well, he told himself, too late to worry about that. He would just have to be careful not to allow these four to learn of his presence, and he would have to look for another opportunity to accomplish his goal.

Then the hunter said something and turned to walk away from the others, but he had gone only a few steps when one of the others called out to him in a louder voice. Hiadeoni thought that he could understand the words, or at least, enough of them to make some sense of what had been said. The language of these Cave People was somewhat like his own.

The man had said something about the hunter coming back later to bring fresh meat, and the hunter had laughed and agreed that he would do so. At least, Hiadeoni thought that was what they had said. The hunter moved off alone again, retracing his steps along the path, and the other three remained there below. Hiadeoni stayed still and watched. The three talked with one another for a moment, then moved off in different directions to conceal themselves. They were guards or sentries, he realized, and he wondered how he had managed to get past them so easily. He had noticed other sentries in other places and had worked his way carefully around them, but these he had not even seen. Somehow he had avoided them without ever knowing that they were there.

He lost sight of the hunter again, and he decided that it was time to move. He eased himself back away from the outcropping, away from the lip of the ledge, and started back the way he had come. He tried to think where he would go if he were the hunter. He would not go back down the side of the mountain toward the roadway below or close to the town. He would move on up to the top of the mountain. And because of the ledge, he would go back to the place where the ledge leveled off and practically converged with the path. Hiadeoni hurried ahead.

Awi-ekwa reached the end of the path and found himself once again on the ridge. He moved to the edge of the trees and stopped. Out there before him, the top of the mountain was a wide, flat, open field. It was a perfect and popular browsing area for deer. Awi-ekwa knew that, as did every other hunter from Stikoyi and Kituwah, but he also knew that the hunters had made too much use of the place, thereby thinning the deer population. Because of that, they had almost ceased hunting there. That had been the case for some time, but for this particular hunt Awi-ekwa thought that they had left it alone long enough. Maybe the deer have come back, he thought.

He waited quietly, and it was not long before his wait was rewarded. Two small female deer cautiously came out into the clearing. They looked around. They moved out a little farther, and then two little ones came out behind them. Still Awi-ekwa waited. Two more adult females moved out into the open. The males could not be far behind, thought Awi-ekwa. He wanted a big, healthy male.

He waited, and then he saw a movement, barely perceptible, along the tree line just behind the small herd. Carefully he nocked an arrow, and he watched intently. A male deer showed itself, stepping out of the trees but staying close to them. It held up its head and looked around, as if standing guard over the browsing herd. It was a good size buck but not as large as Awi-ekwa had been hoping for. He might have to settle for it, he thought. He knew that he was taking a chance coming to this place.

He lifted his bow and was about to draw back the string when he was almost startled by the sudden appearance of a second buck. It stepped out behind the other, and it was big and strong and beautiful. That was the one he wanted. He waited, hoping it would step out farther, but he did not want to wait too long.

It stayed there near the edge of the trees, and Awi-ekwa was afraid to wait anymore. It would be a long shot, but he had made shots like that before. He drew back the string and lined up the shot. Silently he made a small prayer, and then he let the arrow fly. The big buck made a jump forward, then crumpled. The smaller, younger buck bleated out a sudden warning, and the rest of the small herd fled back into the safety of the woods, just as Awi-ekwa pulled out his knife and ran across the clearing to the fallen deer.

He dropped to his knees beside the still form and quickly slit the throat. Then, placing a hand on a warm flank, he offered an apology to Awi-usdi, the spirit chief of all deer.

He had just finished when he heard a slight sound behind him. He was starting to turn and stand all at once, but there was a man already there close behind him, his raised arm already descending. There was no time for Awi-ekwa to react. His mouth opened, but there wasn't even time to call out. The big, ball-headed war club was swift and deadly, and Awi-ekwa was killed instantly when the stone ball crushed his skull.

.   .   .   .

Asquani was mostly hidden in the brush. He was in position to watch the road below, and he could also look back down the mountain path that led to where he and the other two Wolf People were hidden. From where he sat, he could not see either He-Kills-Quickly or Trotting Wolf, but he knew where they were concealed. They were not far away.

They were not hidden for an ambush or even as if lying in wait for game. They were only casually concealed, for their purpose was to watch the road below to make sure that no outsiders came into the land of the Real People. The Real People had been spared the horrors that some of their neighbors, particularly those to the south, had experienced at the hands of the strange white men who had come from somewhere across the waters, the white men that the Real People had come to call *Ani-Asquani*.

Only a few of their people had seen the hairy-faced men, and even fewer had ventured outside their own territory and dealt with the cruel white men face-to-face. These had come back home with tales of terror, and the Real People had decided to isolate themselves from the outside world.

They did not want these *Ani-Asquani* coming into their homes. They discovered that the white men existed in different tribes, and different groups spoke different languages and fought with one another. It was a strange and difficult time, and until the Real People could properly assess the new situation and decide how to effectively deal with it, they would simply stop all strangers who might attempt to venture into their country. They would stop them and tell them to go back, and if the strangers refused to turn around and leave, they would kill them there in the road.

So Asquani, named for the unknown Spaniard who had raped his Timucua mother, Trotting Wolf and He-Kills-Quickly guarded the road that led to the frontier town of Stikoyi. Other members of the Wolf Clan guarded other possible routes into their land. They sat and watched, and their job was mostly boring and tedious, but it was important, and they knew it, and they took it very seriously.

Should they see a party of strangers approaching, a party larger than the three of them could deal with, the fastest one would run along the mountain path and down into the town to call out the others, and a quick ambush would be laid. Everyone knew the procedure.

So 'Squani sat behind his bush, vigilant but not tense.

They had seen no one that day other than the three men they had relieved earlier and the lone hunter, Awi-ekwa. 'Squani had been looking down at the road below. Casually, he glanced back at the mountain path. He saw smoke, a thin wisp like a small campfire. It appeared to be in the path but around a curve so that it was out of their line of sight. He stood up. Still he could see only the curl of rising smoke.

"Trotting Wolf," he said. "Trotting Wolf, can you hear me?"

Trotting Wolf came walking out from behind some boulders. He was staring toward the smoke.

"Yes," he said. "I see it." He raised his voice. "He-Kills-Quickly. Come on out here."

The three guards stood together looking down the path toward the smoke. 'Squani looked toward Trotting Wolf.

"What could it be?" he asked.

"I don't know," said the older man. "Awi-ekwa said he

would come back and cook some meat, but he wouldn't build his fire that far away from us. He knows where we are."

"I'll go take a look," said He-Kills-Quickly.

"I'll go with you," said 'Squani.

"No," said He-Kills-Quickly. "Suppose it's some kind of trap. Better only one is caught in it."

'Squani looked at Trotting Wolf, the senior member of the team.

"He's right," said Trotting Wolf. "We'll wait here until we know what it is." He turned to He-Kills-Quickly. "Be careful," he said.

As they watched He-Kills-Quickly walk away from them, they drew their weapons. Trotting Wolf hefted his war club, and 'Squani drew his Spanish sword, a cherished trophy from an earlier adventure. They waited in tense silence as they watched the other man disappear around a bend in the path.

He-Kills-Quickly saw the fire, but there was something else there too. He couldn't be quite sure just what it was. He walked farther, and he could see that something had been spitted over the fire to cook. Could it be Awi-ekwa after all? But why so far down the path? Then he saw that something was lying prone alongside the fire. No. Two somethings. He squinted, because the shapes were hard to see in the shadow of the overhanging ledge. He thought about going back for the others or just calling out to them, but instead he decided to move in a little closer.

He took a few more steps, and he saw the body of a partially butchered deer. It must be Awi-ekwa, he said to himself. He's cooking the meal he promised us. He walked closer, and then he saw the other body. He couldn't be sure, because the head was bloody, and he wasn't yet close enough for that good a look, but he thought that it was Awi-ekwa. The strange and gruesome scene shocked him into momentary indecision.

He didn't know whether to rush over to check the body or to hurry back down the path for his companions. Then he heard a shout from above, and he looked up toward the ledge. A man stood there, a stranger, and he had a drawn bow in his hands, an arrow nocked and aimed at He-Kills-Quickly.

"I am Hiadeoni of the People of the Great Hill," the stranger shouted. "There is the meal your friend promised you, and now I have kept my promise to the spirit of my uncle, Gana."

He released the string, and the arrow flew straight, driving itself deep into the chest of its target. He-Kills-Quickly was instantly dead, and the figure on the ledge above vanished.

Three

HIADEONI heard them yelling behind him, and
he ran. There were two of them, at least, well
armed and angry. He knew that they would have to climb
up over the ledge before they would be able to really pursue him, so he was confident he could get well away from
them before they could accomplish that. He ran.

He had not known that the guards were up there until
the hunter had spoken to them. That had given them
away. Somehow, he had managed to slip past their guard,
and if he hadn't seen them, there could be others hidden
up there somewhere. The yelling could bring his pursuers
some help. He ran.

A feeling of elation came over Hiadeoni as he ran. He
had made his way alone right into the land of the hated
Cave People in order to avenge the killing of his uncle—a
life for a life. But he had achieved even more than he had
hoped for. However accidentally, he had managed to pene-
trate their guarded passes. He had humiliated them. He

had killed, not just one, but two of them. And then he had cooked their meal for them and left their friend's body there beside it. He ran.

He ran until he was finally certain that no one ran after him, and then he walked. He still kept up a good, brisk pace. He was beyond their borders, but he was still up in the mountains. Far below and to his left, he could see the river, and occasionally he could see the road that ran between the river and the base of the mountain.

He was out of their country, and they had not been able to establish a good pursuit. He was almost sure that they had given up, at least for the present time. They would be taking the bodies down to the village to inform the others there about what had happened to their friends and relatives.

He recalled the day his uncle had been killed. He saw the image of his mother's anguished face. He watched her hack away her long hair in mourning. He heard her wail and scream and sob. And he himself had wept. Many had wept, for Gana had been a much beloved man. He could not recall a more unhappy day in all his life.

Well, he thought, there would be mourning that day in the town of the Cave People. Wives and mothers, nieces and nephews, children and friends, all would be crying that day. The men who were supposed to have guarded the pass would almost certainly be severely criticized, for they had failed, and two lives had been lost.

There would be no further pursuit, he decided. After the mourning, there would be discussion and argument, and eventually someone, probably a relative of one of the dead men, would decide to seek revenge. Then one of the Cave People, or a few of them together, would head for the country of the People of the Great Hill. They would try to kill at least two—two for the two that he had killed. That was the way. It was his way, and it was theirs. It had been thus for many generations.

In a few more days he would be home, and he would tell his people of his success, and they would rejoice. Everyone would be glad that Gana had been properly avenged. But then they would talk about the need to be watchful, for they all would know that there would be an attempt by the Cave People to retaliate. They would prepare themselves, and they would be ready when the time came. The Cave People would not catch them by surprise.

Young Puppy was tired and hungry. He had traveled far from Stikoyi to find his deer. But the deer he had found was not just a deer, but a big deer, and he had killed it. He had bled the animal and gutted it and made the proper prayers. That done, he had strapped it across his shoulders to carry home.

The walk home had been long, especially with the extra weight on his shoulders. He was tired, but he was also in fine, high spirits. He was anxious to get back home to Stikoyi to find out whether his brother had returned. If so, what had he brought with him from his hunt?

He wondered if he might have bested his older brother on his first time out alone by returning home first, or bringing back the biggest kill, or both. That would make it a perfect day.

Of course, if Awi-ekwa was already back and had done as well or better than Young Puppy, the day would not be spoiled. Young Puppy was proud of his older brother, and the competition between them was all in fun. Still, he would dearly love to win the day.

He came at last to the wall around the town of Stikoyi, and he turned to walk through where the ends of the wall overlapped one another to form a narrow entryway. A wide grin spread across his face.

He seemed to get new strength, and he started to trot down the path to his left that would lead him to his mother's house. Close to the house, he shouted in his exuberance.

"*Etsi,*" he called. "Mother. Are you home? It's Young Puppy coming home from the hunt. Is my big brother back yet?"

No one answered him. The house was just around the turn in the road.

"Is Awi-ekwa back?" he shouted, and just then he rounded the curve, and he saw the house, and he saw the small crowd gathered there, and he knew that something was terribly wrong. He stopped. Then he walked forward slowly. At the edge of the crowd, he lowered his burden. He made his way through the crowd. When the people saw who it was, they moved aside to let him through. Then he saw the body lying there, matted blood on the side of the crushed, misshapen head. He gasped. He fell to his knees, and he started to cry, shamelessly, wailing out loud for the whole town to hear.

No one yet talked of revenge. No one asked just how the two deaths had occurred. The bodies had to be prepared, the funeral ceremony given and the time of mourning completed. Nothing could interfere with that. The souls of the two lost men had to be properly sent on their way to the Darkening Land. That done, there would be time enough for talking and for planning.

Seven days had passed since his brother had been killed before Young Puppy went to see Trotting Wolf. On the day he chose to visit with the Wolf Clan leader, Trotting Wolf was again on the mountain, guarding the pass with other Wolves. Young Puppy made the same climb that his brother had made on that fatal day. He walked down the same path, passing over the very place where the killer had built the taunting campfire and laid out the body.

Young Puppy found Trotting Wolf just about where Awi-ekwa had found him seven days earlier. With Trotting Wolf, again, was Asquani. There were four others there too. Following the success of the lone Senika, they had strengthened the guard. Trotting Wolf and Asquani came out to talk with Young Puppy.

"I came to ask you," said Young Puppy, "if you are planning to do anything about the killings of my brother and the other man."

He wore an angry sulk on his face. Of course, thought Trotting Wolf, he had reason to be angry, but he also had the impatience of youth, a thing always difficult to deal with.

"Yes, of course we are," he said. "I know you're in a hurry, but these things shouldn't be rushed."

"My brother is dead," said Young Puppy. "I don't care how long you and the other Wolf People wait. I'm going north to kill some *Ani-Senika.*"

"And so am I," said 'Squani. "But I'm also taking the

advice of Trotting Wolf. He's wise in these matters. Listen to him."

Young Puppy cocked his head to one side, giving Trotting Wolf a suspicious look.

"When that Senika man left here," said Trotting Wolf, "he ran home to tell his people what he had done."

"To brag about it," said Young Puppy.

"Yes. Of course," said Trotting Wolf. "And what do you suppose the rest of the *Ani-Senika* thought when they heard?"

"They probably thought that he was a great man. They probably rejoiced and made a feast and dance."

"Yes, certainly," said Trotting Wolf, "but what else?"

Young Puppy looked puzzled. He looked at the ground between himself and Trotting Wolf, and nervously shuffled his feet.

"Well, I don't know," he said.

"Do you suppose that the *Ani-Senika* believe that the Real People don't care when someone kills our own?" asked Trotting Wolf. "Do they think that they can do that, and we'll just stay home, sitting on our hands?"

"Why, no. I think that they should know us better than that," said Young Puppy. "We've killed enough of them in the past."

"Then what must they have thought when this man came home? What must they be thinking now about the future?"

"Oh," said Young Puppy. "I see what you mean. They must be thinking that some of us will come up to their country to seek revenge."

"Exactly," said the Wolf Clan leader. "And so they must be planning for it. They would have gotten themselves ready right away, and they will be watching for us, ready to defend themselves. So if we had rushed right on up there, we would probably have run into an ambush and gotten ourselves killed. Wouldn't we? And if we rush up now, it still might happen."

"Well," said Young Puppy. "Yes. I suppose so. I guess you're right. But when—"

"So we wait for a little while," interrupted the older man, growing a little impatient with the hotheaded youth. "We give them enough time to relax. We allow them to think that maybe we're not coming after all. Then we go, and we catch them by surprise."

"How much longer then," asked Young Puppy, "do you think that I should wait?"

Trotting Wolf walked away and stared down at the road below. Then he turned back to face Asquani.

"What do you think, little brother?" he asked. "How soon will you begin this journey?"

"Another seven days, I think," said 'Squani.

"That soon?"

"Yes. I think they'd expect us immediately, and if we don't show up immediately, then they'll be expecting us to take a good long while to prepare—a month or maybe more. Fourteen days plus the time it takes to get there will surprise them, I think."

"Well, you may be right," said Trotting Wolf. He glanced back at Young Puppy. "Have you ever made a trip like this before?" he asked. "Have you killed an enemy?"

Young Puppy looked at the ground for a moment in embarrassed silence.

"No," he said. "But everyone has to have a first time."

"Of course. I was just thinking that you should go with

someone rather than by yourself. Do you even know the way to the land of the *Ani-Senika?*"

"I could find it by myself," said Young Puppy, "if I have to."

"I'm sure you could, but it's a long trip," said 'Squani. "So far, no one else has offered to go with me. I'd be happy to have some company and some help on this journey."

Young Puppy looked at 'Squani with wide eyes that betrayed his gladness and surprise at hearing that welcome offer. He would never admit it to anyone, but he had been apprehensive, afraid that he might be killed without having properly avenged his brother.

"It's a good idea," said Trotting Wolf. "One of the men killed here was a Wolf Person. 'Squani will go for him. The other was your brother, a—"

"A Long Hair Person," said Young Puppy.

"Yes," said Trotting Wolf. "And you will go for the Long Hairs—and your brother. That's as it should be. Now you have seven days to prepare yourself for this journey. Do you know what to do?"

"Yes," said Young Puppy. "I think so."

"Get your weapons together and in good shape. Ask your mother to prepare some trail food for you. Fast and pray the last four days."

"Just as the sun appears in the morning sky on the seventh day from now," said 'Squani, "I'll meet you right here, and we'll begin our journey together."

"I'll be here," said Young Puppy, "and I'll be ready to go."

Four

YOUNG PUPPY sat on a split log bench in front of his mother's house, leaning back against the wall. He had just finished the meal she had prepared for him and his father. They were quiet, for only a few days had passed since the death of Awi-ekwa. The funeral was over, and so was the open, public mourning, but it was still somber and quiet around the house of Lolo. Young Puppy had not yet told her of his intention to seek revenge for the killing of his brother. He knew that he would have to tell her, for soon he would have to begin his preparations.

"Mother," he said. "The meal was good."

"I'm glad you liked it," she said, but she gave him an inquisitive look, for something in the tone of his voice indicated to her that he wanted to tell her something more serious than that. Neither of her sons had ever been able to fool her or keep anything from her. Both of them had always told her everything.

Bear Meat, or Yona-hawiya, her husband, also gave his

son a puzzled look. He too had noticed the sound of the voice. Young Puppy looked up nervously. He read the knowing expressions on the faces of his parents, and he knew that it was time to tell them about his plans.

"I'm going on a trip to the north," he said. "I don't know how long I'll be gone. Asquani's going with me. You know Asquani from Kituwah? He's going for the Wolf People. I'm going—for my brother."

There was a long and uncomfortable pause. Then Bear Meat spoke up to break the silence. He knew what his wife must be thinking, but he thought that it would best be left unsaid.

"You're going up to the Senika country?" he asked.

"Yes," said Young Puppy, his eyes cast down to avoid looking at either of his parents.

"That's good," said Bear Meat, and he gave his wife a look. "That's as it should be. It's your place, and you're old enough. And 'Squani is a good man, I think. I've heard the stories about him. He's been through some tough fights, and he knows how to take care of himself."

"Do you know him?" asked Young Puppy.

"No, but I've seen him, and I've heard the stories about his adventures," said Bear Meat. "His father was a white man, a 'squani. Potmaker, his mother, a Timucua woman, was captured by the whites. They raped her. Several of them. So his father was one of those Ani-Asquani. No one knows which one. Anyhow, that's how he got that name."

"Then how did he come to be a Real Person," asked Young Puppy, "and a Wolf?"

"Carrier, from Kituwah, went south to trade. He rescued Potmaker from the white men and brought her home to be his wife. Asquani was born in Kituwah, and his mother was adopted by the Wolves."

"Someone told me that he wanted to become a real *'squani* one time," said Young Puppy. "Just like his real father."

"Yes," said Bear Meat. "Of course, I've heard that tale as well. He ran away from his home in the night and traveled east to the Dark Island on the edge of the big water. The whites were building a settlement there. They intended to stay. Asquani went to live with them and learn their ways. But he found out that all the things he had been told about their cruelty were true, so he turned against them and helped to wipe them out and run them off the island for good."

"He still carries a big metal knife," said Young Puppy. "I saw him with it."

"Yes. A Spanish sword," said Bear Meat. "He must have got it in the fighting there. Yes. He'll be a good one for you to go with on your first time, I think. Watch him and listen to him and you'll learn much."

"You be careful," said Lolo. She had kept quiet for a long time, but she could no longer hold her tongue. "It won't be Asquani I'll be worrying about. I don't want to lose two sons. Be careful."

Young Puppy stood up and walked close to his mother. He could see the worry in her eyes, and he thought that he could understand her feelings. She was, after all, still grieving over the loss of her oldest son. Well, he was too. He was grieving the loss of his only brother, and though he didn't want to cause his mother further grief and pain, he had to do something to make it right.

"I will, Mother," he said. "Don't worry about me. Asquani will be with me. He's one of the Wolves who guard the pass. I'll be careful, and I'll get revenge for my brother, and I'll come safely back home to you. You can be sure of that."

She wished that she could be as sure as he. She didn't think that she could stand the loss of both her sons. She longed to tell him that he couldn't go, that she wouldn't allow it, but she knew that it would do no good. He was too old to hold back. She thought about her boys when they were little. The years had gone by too quickly. Oh well, she'd have to let him go. She felt a tear dampen her eye, and she turned away so that the others would not see.

Asquani, the Spaniard, lay naked under the bear robe in the home of his wife Osa, the Catawba woman he had rescued from the Spaniards and then married. She was under there with him, but she was still asleep. It was early morning. He was anxious for her to wake up, for he had some things to tell her, but she looked so peaceful lying there that he decided he would not disturb her slumber. He would wait.

He crawled out from under the bearskin, carefully, so he would not awaken Osa, and he started to dress himself. He heard her moan softly, and he turned just in time to see her roll over onto her back under the cover. Her eyes were still shut. His own eyes studied the soft features of her face for a moment before moving on down to the mound of her belly. It was obvious, even covered as it was by the thick bearskin. She was going to have an *usdi*. Just the thought of it filled him with excitement. He would be· a father.

He decided that she needed her strength. She needed all the rest that she could get, and so he would let her sleep as

long as she could. The other people in town would be
going to the water already, and he decided to go with
them. Quietly, he left the house.

He was one of the last of the residents of Kituwah to
reach the edge of the river, and he quickly stripped and
waded in. The water was cold, coming down from the high
mountains, even in the middle of the hottest part of the
year with the sun, old Sol, beating down from overhead.
Sol. That was what the sun was called by the *Ani-Asquani*.
Although he had learned to hate his unknown father's people, he still cherished his knowledge of their language, and
he often spoke it in his mind to keep the knowledge alive.

He and Young Puppy, he thought, would have to make
their journey north a successful one, for soon the weather
would be against them in that cold land of the *Ani-Senika*.
He came back out of the water, thankful for a strong sun in
which to dry himself. He pulled on his leggings and fastened his breechclout in place. Then he went to find his
mother.

He spoke to several people as he made his way along the
river's edge, and when he came to the place where his
mother, Potmaker, and his adopted father, Carrier, had
come out of the water with his young baby sister, their
daughter, he found them dressed and ready to go back to
Potmaker's house.

"Where's your wife this morning?" Potmaker asked
him.

"I left her sleeping," said 'Squani. "Maybe she needs
more sleep because of the little one."

"Yes. You're probably right," said his mother. "Do you
want to come home with us to eat?"

"I think I should go back first to see if my wife is awake yet."

"All right," said Potmaker, "but if she is awake, come along anyway and bring her with you. You can both eat with us."

"All three of you can eat with us," said Carrier.

They laughed at Carrier's good-natured joke, as Carrier picked up his little daughter.

"All right," said 'Squani. "I will. I'll bring them both with me."

They all started walking back toward the houses. 'Squani walked along with them.

"I'll be taking a trip soon," he said. "I'm going to the land of the *Ani-Senika*. I'm going for the Wolf People."

"You're going because of what happened to those two men up on the mountain?" asked Carrier.

"Yes."

"Alone?" asked Potmaker.

"No. Not alone. Young Puppy, the brother of the Long Hair man who was killed—he's going with me."

"Young Puppy sounds like the name of a boy," said Carrier, "one who has not done anything to earn a man's name. It could be dangerous to make such a trip with one so inexperienced. What do you know of him?"

"Not much," admitted 'Squani. "He came to Trotting Wolf and said he was going to go by himself. He's very angry about his brother. Don't worry. I'll watch him closely. I'll be careful. Maybe he'll earn a new name for himself on this trip."

"Just be sure that you're not so busy watching Young Puppy that you forget to watch the *Ani-Senika*," said Carrier.

They came to the turning where 'Squani left them to go back to the house of his wife.

"I'll be along shortly," he said, "with Osa—and our little one. Make sure you have enough for all of us to eat."

He found her up, dressed and combing her hair. When he walked into the house, she looked up at him. He thought how big and beautiful her eyes were. She smiled at him softly.

"You let me sleep too long," she said. "Have you already been to the water?"

"Yes," he said, noticing again how well she was getting along in her new language, the language of the Real People. Osa was a Catawba. She had been a captive of the Spaniards on the Dark Island, and 'Squani had taken her with him when he ran away. Like him, she could speak the language of the hairy-faced men, and her name, Osa, was Spanish for she-bear. He had never figured out just why they had given her that name. "It's all right, though," he continued. "You probably needed to sleep. My mother said that I was right not to wake you up. She has invited us to her house to eat."

"Well then," said Osa, "I'll be ready right away."

He sat down on the bearskin and watched her working on her hair. She was a beautiful woman, and he was a very lucky man to have her. But he had some news that she had to know about, and though he hated to tell her, he had already told his mother. It couldn't wait any longer.

"Osa," he said, "I'm going on a trip. A long trip. To the land of the *Ani-Senika.*"

He waited for a reaction, but she just kept combing her long, beautiful hair. He stood up and paced across to the far wall.

"You know that Senika man killed two Real People," he said. "One of them was a Long Hair Person. His younger brother, Young Puppy, from Stikoyi, will go with me for the Long Hair People. The other was a Wolf Person, and I'm going for the Wolf People."

"Why are you the one?" she asked.

"Young Puppy has no experience in these matters," he said. "Someone with experience has to go with him."

"There are others with experience—even more than you. There's Trotting Wolf and the Howler."

"Yes," he said. "That's true. But I volunteered to go. Once, I had no clan. I was not even a Real Person until the Wolf People made me one of their own. Now a Wolf Person has been killed by a Senika man. I must go, Osa. Without the Wolf People, we would have no home, you and I. Do you understand?"

She put aside her comb and stood to face him, and she smiled.

"Yes," she said. "I understand, but I'll miss you very much while you're gone, and I'll worry about you. Be careful, and come home safely to me—and to our little one."

"I will," he said. "I have too much to live for now to let some Senika take it all away from me."

He thought about the time before he had met Osa, and the time before the Wolf People had adopted his mother and himself. Back then he would never have believed that he would be so happy and content. Back then he hadn't even thought he had a home. He almost chuckled to recall the foolish desperation which had driven him to search out the Spaniards, looking for a place to belong.

"Well," said Osa, putting down her comb, "right now, we'd better get on over to your mother's house."

Five

THEY MET at the appointed time and place. It was early in the morning. The sun had not yet shown her face, though her light was beginning to color the sky along the eastern horizon. Young Puppy was anxious to get going, and Asquani realized right away that he was going to have to teach this young man to pace himself and encourage him to develop his patience. They had a long trip ahead of them, and there was no sense in wearing themselves out at the beginning. He knew there would be plenty of time for teaching along the way.

As they moved along the first day, rather than say anything to Young Puppy about his haste and his youthful exuberance, Asquani simply traveled at an easy pace. Young Puppy had to constantly slow himself down and wait for Asquani to catch up with him. He tried to hide his exasperation with the older, slower man, but it showed right through. His brow was knit. The corners of his mouth slightly turned down. 'Squani recognized these signs, smiled to himself and said nothing.

It was not yet dark when 'Squani selected a good spot to camp for the night. He could tell that Young Puppy was aggravated with him and probably wanted to say something, but the younger man managed to keep his thoughts to himself until after they had eaten. The sun was low in the western sky, but still there was light. There would be for a while. Young Puppy stood staring toward the north. He paced. At last he could stand it no longer, and he spoke.

"It's still early," said Young Puppy, "and I'm not even tired. Why did we stop so soon? We could have gone farther today."

"Yes," said 'Squani, "we could have gone on a little farther, but this is a good place to camp. Farther on, we might not have found such a good place as this. We would not want to still be searching for a campsite after the sky is dark."

"Huh," said Young Puppy. What 'Squani had said made sense, but he was still not satisfied. "We moved slowly all day long," he said.

Young Puppy's face had developed a definite pout by this time, and 'Squani had to control himself to keep from smiling at it. He understood. He was not really all that much older than Young Puppy, and he could remember well the years of his own youthful exuberance.

"You've never made a long trip like this before," he said, "have you?"

"No, but I—"

"Well, I know," said 'Squani, "that it seems to you that we didn't travel as far today as we could have, but you

don't want to wear yourself out right at the very beginning
of a long trip like this one. Be patient, Young Puppy. If we
pace ourselves well, and if we're careful—and patient—
we'll not only arrive at our destination, but we'll also accomplish our purpose. I know you're anxious. You're still
angry. But you also have much to learn."

Young Puppy did not seem to take the advice well, but
'Squani was not worried about him. His brother had been
killed, and it was natural for him to react in that way. The
long trip would force some patience on him and cool his
anger some. He seemed capable and bright enough.
'Squani thought that he would be all right by the time they
reached their destination. He settled down and slept well
through the night.

Young Puppy, on the other hand, did not sleep well. He
seethed with anger, impatience and humiliation. 'Squani
had slowed him down all day, stopped early when they still
had good traveling time ahead of them and then had lec-
tured him as if he were a mere boy. He slept fitfully, toss-
ing this way and that, until far into the night.

When Young Puppy was at last fast asleep, the sun was just
beginning to light the far eastern horizon. He felt something shake him by the shoulder, and he awoke abruptly to
see 'Squani looking down at him.

"What?" he said. "What is it?"

"It's time to be up and on our way," said 'Squani. "The
sun is coming out. The day's begun."

Young Puppy wanted to go back to sleep, but he did not
dare say so. He had complained the night before about
wasting daylight and traveling time. He prepared himself
to travel as quickly as he could, but for most of that day, he

felt as if he were trying to walk in his sleep. In contrast to the previous day, he found himself having a difficult time keeping up with his traveling companion. He struggled to keep it from showing. That evening, when 'Squani found a campsite and finally decided to stop, Young Puppy did not complain. He was secretly grateful, and that night, he did not toss and turn in his sleep. He slept soundly and well.

The third day, Young Puppy and Asquani traveled at more or less the same speed, and by the middle of the fourth day, Young Puppy had adjusted to the pace and the schedule. The two men were moving along well together. It was then they saw a thin wisp of smoke up ahead that appeared to be in their path. They stopped.

"A campfire?" said Young Puppy.

"I think so," said Asquani.

"What will we do?"

Asquani studied the terrain ahead. They were walking along a well-used trail which ran nearly parallel to a small river. The river ran from north to south and was off to their right. To their left, rocky tree-covered hillsides rose up steeply. The thin line of rising smoke appeared to be coming from a spot up ahead, probably beside the river, but the actual campsite, if that's what it was, was hidden from their vision by the road, the river and the hillside, which all curved sharply to the left. Should they continue walking along the road, they might come face-to-face with campers who could be unfriendly to them.

'Squani looked up the side of the steep hill to his left. To someone from the flatlands, it might have appeared to be a difficult climb, but the Real People were mountain people born and bred.

"Let's go up there," he said, and without waiting for a

reply, he started to lead the way. The brush on the hillside was thick, and it was a steep climb, but 'Squani soon discovered an almost natural pathway lined with rocks to serve both as handholds and as steps. About halfway up the hillside, they came upon a kind of shelf. It was wide enough to use as a trail for one man at a time, and it seemed to run around the hillside, almost level with the ground below. 'Squani led the way, and Young Puppy followed close behind.

At last they were able to see the camp clearly down below. As they had surmised, it was located on the near bank of the river. They moved into position to get a good look at the people in the camp, and Young Puppy was astonished, almost frightened, by what he saw, for never in his life had he seen such a sight: white men and *sogwilis*. Asquani too was surprised, for he recognized one of the men immediately. It was his old friend, Jacques Tournier. He took a moment to look the others over, and he knew them all.

"Those are white men," said Young Puppy. "*Ani-Asquani?*"

"They're white men, all right," said 'Squani, "but they're not *Ani-Asquani*. They come from a different tribe. These men call themselves *Français*. Their leader, the one standing there near the fire with the long white feather in his hat, is called Jacques Tournier."

"You know these white men?" said Young Puppy.

"Yes, I do. They're the ones who helped us drive the *Ani-Asquani* off the Dark Island," said 'Squani. "The *Ani-Asquani* are their enemies as well as ours. Let's go down and talk to them."

·   ·   ·   ·

Tournier and the other five Frenchmen, as well as their native guide and interpreter, recognized 'Squani almost at once. 'Squani introduced them to Young Puppy, speaking through the interpreter, Little Black Bear, a Catawba. 'Squani and Little Black Bear conversed in the trade language. Tournier and his company seemed genuinely happy to see 'Squani again, and to meet Young Puppy.

Fresh venison was cooking, and Tournier invited the two *Chalaques*, as he called them, to eat. The two Real People were happy to have a good hot meal, for they had eaten nothing but *gahawista*, their parched corn trail food, for several days. Their meal done, they talked.

"Well, *mon ami*," said Tournier, speaking through Little Black Bear, "it's been a while since we fought the good fight together against the *Espagnols*. It's good to see you again. Is the country of your people still closed to all outsiders?"

"Yes," said 'Squani, "it is. The Wolves still guard the passes to keep everyone out."

"I know," said Tournier, "that you and others of your people have had some very bad experiences with those brutal *Espagnols*. All of you *Indiens* in this part of this great land of yours have ample reason to hate them and beware of them. But we are not like the *Espagnols*. They are my enemies too, and enemies of my king. We *Français* would like to be your friends."

"Of course, I know that," said 'Squani, "but most of the Real People are still cautious. They're not sure they should trust any white-skinned man. It will take some time to convince them."

"*Oui*," said Tournier. "I dare say. And I can't blame

them any for their caution. So what is it that brings you two so far away from your homes?"

'Squani knew that Tournier was establishing relationships with various tribes of native people in order to establish trade relations, but he did not know how many different peoples the Frenchman had made contact with. For all he knew, Tournier might have just concluded some kind of friendly arrangement with the Senika People. Therefore, he felt that he should answer the Frenchman's question carefully.

"Young Puppy and I are on our way to a place north of here to see some . . . people we know," he said. "And we had better be on our way now. We have a long journey ahead of us yet. The food was good, and so was the visit. *Wado.*"

He stood up, and Young Puppy followed his lead. Tournier came quickly to his own feet in response. He did not want to lose touch with these *Chalaques*, but he knew that he couldn't interfere with their business, whatever it was. He glanced over at his small herd of horses grazing contentedly beside the water, and he made a quick decision he thought would probably pay off well in the end.

"*Mon ami,*" he said. "You have a long road ahead of you, and you are walking. *Non?* How would you like to have two of these fine *chevaux* on which to ride? It will make your travel both easier and swifter."

'Squani had learned to ride while he had been with the Spaniards on the Dark Island, and he knew that he could teach Young Puppy quickly. The *sogwilis* would make their trip much faster.

"We have nothing to trade for them," he said.

"If you want them," said Tournier, "they're yours. A gift

from me to you. A friend to a friend. Well, what do you say?"

'Squani smiled and took the Frenchman's hand.

"Yes," he said. "Thank you."

Tournier saw the looks on the faces of the other Frenchmen, and he knew that, at best, they were puzzled that he would give two good horses away to these traveling *Indiens*. And nothing in exchange.

Ah well, he thought, they don't have to approve of my decisions. They had brought extra horses along in case of any unforeseen difficulties, and Tournier wanted badly to get inside the country of the Real People and establish an alliance with them. Two horses, he thought, would be a small price to pay for the good will of these powerful southern people.

They even had a couple of extra French saddles, so Tournier had two men saddle two good mounts and deliver them into the hands of 'Squani and Young Puppy. Young Puppy was afraid of the large beast at first, but he watched 'Squani ride safely. Then both 'Squani and Tournier instructed him in how to ride the animal, teaching him how to control it with the reins and with his knees. Although Young Puppy fell off a time or two and was laughed at heartily by the Frenchmen, he tried his best to laugh with them each time, as he remounted to continue his lessons.

By the time he was riding competently, it was late afternoon, and Tournier invited the two Real People to spend the night at his camp.

"You'll more than make up for the lost time now that you have these *chevaux*," he said.

'Squani declined politely. He knew that Tournier was right about the time, of course, but he did not want to leave himself in the position of having to make conversation with these men. They might ask more questions about his destination. By the time the sun was low in the western sky, and they stopped to make their own camp, he and Young Puppy were well away from the camp of the white men.

Six

MOVING about the campsite that night, Young Puppy found that the insides of his legs were very sore and tender to the touch. He was limping, although he was trying not to let it show. He worried that he would not be able to run and fight when they reached the land of the *Ani-Senika*. 'Squani noticed the limping, but he did not say anything. He remembered the first time he had ridden a *sogwili*. He pretended not to notice.

At last 'Squani stretched out on the ground to sleep for the night, and Young Puppy prepared to do the same. As he crouched toward the ground, a sharp pain shot through his legs, and he groaned out loud in spite of himself. He managed to get himself down and stretch out his body. He heaved a long and heavy sigh. If 'Squani did not know already, he thought, he knows now.

" 'Squani," he said. "Do your legs hurt?"

"Yes," said 'Squani. "They hurt me a little. It's been a while since I rode a *sogwil'*."

"I never rode one before, and my legs are killing me."

"They'll get better as you ride more," 'Squani said. "Soon they won't hurt you at all."

"Will they be all right by the time we reach the Senika country?"

"Yes," said 'Squani. "I think they will."

Young Puppy rolled onto his side, groaned once more, and rolled to the other side, trying to find a position where the pain wouldn't keep him awake. He tossed around like that for a while, hoping desperately that Asquani was right about getting used to the riding. When he at last fell asleep, he rode hard through his dreams for the rest of the night.

In the morning, 'Squani saddled his mount and helped Young Puppy to saddle his. A couple more times, he thought, and Young Puppy would no longer need any help. He was a fast learner. They mounted up and started on their way. It was an uneventful day of travel.

When they stopped at the end of that day, Young Puppy was surprised to find that, even though they had ridden longer and farther than the day before, his legs did not hurt him as much as they had the night before. After three more days of riding, they did not hurt him at all. He was saddling the *sogwili* without help from Asquani, and he was riding comfortably and skillfully. It made him feel good and proud.

Young Puppy actually enjoyed riding the *sogwili*. They were traveling much farther in a day than they would have on foot, and it gave him a wonderful feeling of freedom to race across the land. Now and then, when the countryside was flat and open, Asquani would allow them to do just that. He had told Young Puppy, though, that they could not force the animals to run hard for very long at a time. This he had learned from the *Ani-Asquani.*

Much of the time they rode in silence, and Young Puppy's thoughts during these times were often of doing great deeds. He saw himself as a mounted warrior, striking fear into the very hearts of the enemies of the Real People.

But he also thought of his initial impression of Asquani at the start of their journey. Young Puppy admitted to himself that he had been very wrong about his companion —his new friend. He had learned a great deal already from Asquani, and he thought that he would almost certainly learn much more before the journey was done.

The thoughts of Asquani were quite different. He had been watching his young companion and getting acquainted with him. He was, of course, concerned about the way Young Puppy would perform when they actually faced their enemy. That was important. A foolish man could get both himself and his companion killed by his carelessness. And he remembered well the warnings of Carrier about that subject.

But 'Squani was beginning to feel confident that Young Puppy would do well. He had developed some patience, he had endurance, and his anger had cooled. All that was significant. And the young man was skillful and quick to learn. He had also demonstrated, after those first few days of youthful stubbornness, that he was willing to listen to his older and more experienced companion. He was beginning to think that Young Puppy would be just fine. And he liked the young man.

But 'Squani had other thoughts too. When a man went out on a trip with a mission like the one they were charged with, no matter how skillful or experienced he might be, there was always a chance that he would not see home again. 'Squani was not afraid to die, although, of course, he had much to live for. He knew that his wife and child would be cared for by the Bird People, the clan that had adopted her, should anything happen to him.

But then, he had another worry. There was the writing. His adopted father, Carrier, had taught him how to write the language of the Real People. He had told him that it must remain a secret for a while, but that it was important that it not be lost. If something were to happen to 'Squani, then Carrier would have to find someone else to teach. And he knew that same concern was bothering Carrier at home.

So 'Squani studied Young Puppy, not only because of the upcoming battle. He studied the young man wondering whether or not he should trust the knowledge of the writing to him. Carrier had said that he would one day select someone. At the end of another day of riding, they camped. They slept the night and were up with the sun, and 'Squani had decided. He should. And he would.

"Young Puppy," he said.

The young man turned toward 'Squani. He had thought that they were about ready to start riding again.

"Have you heard about the *Ani-Kutani?*" said Asquani.

Young Puppy gave his older companion a quizzical look. What kind of question, he wondered, was that to be asking at such a time?

"Yes," he said. "I've heard stories about the old-time priests. They were all killed."

"They were *almost* all killed," 'Squani corrected. "At the

time the people rose up against them, there were two who were still alive, away somewhere in the west."

"Oh yes," said Young Puppy. "I remember that part of the story. Three of the priests had been sent west on a journey. They were captured by some people out there, and one of them was killed right away. One returned home just after the people had attacked Men's Town, the town where all the priests stayed, and they let him live."

"That's right," said 'Squani, "and the other was eventually sold to the *Ani-Asquani*. He was with them a long time before he came back to us. I knew him. He was the oldest of the three. He taught me to speak the language of the *Ani-Asquani*."

Young Puppy just nodded. He had also heard the tales about Asquani, the half Spaniard who had run away to live with the cruel white men but had returned to the Real People when he learned just how cruel they were. Riding all this time with 'Squani on this special mission, Young Puppy had almost forgotten all that. Now he wondered just what this strange Real Person was up to. Why had he brought up these old tales?

"The other priest," said 'Squani, "is still alive. At least, the last I knew he was still living in Ijodi. He's an old man, and he is known as Dancing Rabbit because of the way he escaped from his captors out in the west. He sang the rabbit song and danced the rabbit dance just as Jisdu did in the story of his escape from the wolves."

"Oh yes," said Young Puppy. "I've heard all that too. But why are we talking about it now? Shouldn't we be riding on?"

"We will soon," said 'Squani. "Dancing Rabbit thought that he was the last living *Kutani*. And now he is, of course, for the other one has gone. Anyway, he was afraid, and may still be, that someone would decide to kill him too."

"But they didn't," said Young Puppy.

"No, they didn't. They let him live. And he was living with a terrible secret."

"What was that?"

"Have you ever heard—"

'Squani stopped himself and thought for a moment. He thought about Carrier's cautions regarding the writing. Still it could be dangerous to let anyone know about it. But his decision had been made.

"I have his secret," he said, "but I can't tell you about it until you've promised to keep it. No one else can know."

Young Puppy's face suddenly took on a worried look.

"You said that it was a terrible secret," he said.

"Yes," said 'Squani.

"Does that mean that it's dangerous to know?"

"Yes, but it's also very important."

Young Puppy sat and stared at the ground for a long moment of silence. Then he looked up at 'Squani.

"If you want to tell me," he said, "if you want to trust me with this terrible and important secret, I'll keep it to myself. No one will ever hear it from me."

"Only one," said 'Squani, "someday. Just as I have chosen you to pass this information along to, someday you'll have to choose a young man to tell. I told you that it's important. So even though we must keep it secret, we can't let it die. Do you understand?"

"Yes."

"The secret of Dancing Rabbit," said 'Squani, "was that he knew how to write our language. When he was a *Kutani*, he was a scribe."

"Oh yes," said Young Puppy. "I think I've heard about that. Not a real story about it. Just that those old-time priests could do that. That they had some magic way of marking down words."

"Not magic," said 'Squani. "It's something that anyone can learn. Let me show you."

He dropped down on his knees, smoothed a place in the dirt and with a stick, drew a symbol.

"You see that?" he asked.

"Yes. Of course."

"Every time you see just this symbol, you make the sound of ah."

"Ah," said Young Puppy.

"Now you write it."

Young Puppy took the stick and copied the symbol.

"Ah," he said.

"That's right."

Then 'Squani drew the symbol for the hissing sound, and he placed it just to the right of the first symbol. He made the sound, and Young Puppy repeated it.

"Now say them both together," said Asquani.

"Ahss," said Young Puppy, and he copied the second symbol. Asquani drew a third and said, "Qua." Again Young Puppy copied the symbol and said the sounds out loud in sequence. Finally Asquani finished the word he was writing with one final symbol.

"This one has the sound of ni," he said.

Young Puppy copied that one, and then he read again.

"Ah-s-qua-ni," he said. "Asquani. It's your name."

"Yes. You see? There's no magic. It's only something you can learn. There are many more symbols, but once you've learned them all, you can write down anything you can say. And someone else who also knows the symbols can read your words."

"But then," said Young Puppy, "why is it a terrible secret? Why is it so dangerous?"

"Because many of the people still have bad feelings about the *Ani-Kutani*, and if they knew about this, they might kill us, for fear that we're harboring other secrets and perhaps other powers—magic, as you said yourself—of the *Ani-Kutani*. They would kill us for knowing this, because they would be afraid of us."

"I think I understand," said Young Puppy, "but if we can't make use of it, if we can't tell everyone about it, then what good is it to us?"

"It's no good to us just now," 'Squani answered, "but someday, when the memory of the *Ani-Kutani* has faded, the person who knows it will then be able to teach it again, this time to all of the Real People. So I'll teach you all of the symbols, and in secret, you can practice them so you don't forget them. Then one day, you will choose a younger person to pass it along to, telling him everything that I've told you."

"Yes," said Young Puppy. "I will."

"Remember just these four for now," said 'Squani, "and let's get on our way."

Young Puppy stared at the symbols there before him for another moment, then suddenly rubbed them out.

"I'm ready," he said, and he stood up and walked toward the horses. 'Squani watched him for a moment, feeling good, thinking that he had indeed made the right decision. Young Puppy picked up a saddle and swung it into place. 'Squani stood up and followed.

Seven

ASQUANI couldn't be sure, but he thought that they had reached the land of the *Ani-Quanuhgi*. They would have to be careful. The Real People had not had any recent problems with the *Ani-Quanuhgi*, but they were not on friendly terms with them either. Though the two peoples had not sent parties into one another's territory for many months, they fought anytime they happened upon one another.

In moving through this country, Asquani realized that there was, after all, a disadvantage to traveling on the back of a *sogwili*. The big animals could not travel through the woods and on the mountainsides the way a man on foot could. They had to stay on the roads, or on reasonably wide paths through the woods or in open country. He cautioned Young Puppy to stay alert.

"Riding on these animals," he said, "we might easily be seen by an enemy before we see him."

"Yes. Of course, you're right," said Young Puppy. "Or heard. They're not so quiet either."

The sun was high overhead. She had almost reached her daughter's house in the center of the underside of the great Sky Vault when the road left the mountains and trees and started to cross a vast open prairie. 'Squani looked back at Young Puppy, who had been riding just a short distance behind him.

"This would be a good time, I think," he said, "to let the *sogwilis* run for a short distance."

"All right," said Young Puppy.

'Squani lightly kicked his mount in the sides, and it seemed to leap forward, anxious to be allowed to stretch its legs in a good run. Young Puppy did the same. As his animal picked up speed, he decided to turn the little run into a race, and he managed to pull up alongside 'Squani, and then he moved ahead just a little. It was a great feeling, moving across the land at such speed. He looked at 'Squani, and both men smiled. They raced on for a time, and then 'Squani called out to Young Puppy, "*Elikwa*. It's enough."

They pulled back on the reins to slow the *sogwilis* back down to a walk.

"Do we stop and let them rest?" asked Young Puppy.

"No," said 'Squani. "Not yet. After they run hard, they should walk for a while."

He looked ahead, and he could see the beginning of the woods again on the far edge of the prairie they were crossing.

"I see trees over there," he said. "When we get there we can rest a little."

They were about halfway to the trees when Young
Puppy saw some movement ahead just at the edge of the
woods.

" 'Squani," he said, "I think there are some men up
there."

"Where?" said 'Squani.

"Just at the edge of the trees. Almost directly in front of
us."

Side by side, they rode on slowly and in silence, neither
one giving any indication of having seen or suspected anything. Each man watched the trees ahead for any signs.

"Yes," said 'Squani. "I see one now."

"I see two," said Young Puppy.

"Five now," said 'Squani.

"Even more. Eight, at least."

The men seemed to be moving, more or less abreast, out
of the trees to the edge of the clearing. They were armed
and painted, and they stayed close to the trees once they
had shown themselves.

"They're waiting for us," said 'Squani.

They rode closer, to a spot just a little too far for a bow
shot, and 'Squani stopped his mount. Young Puppy
stopped just beside him. The men at the tree line had not
moved any farther out from the trees.

"Do you know who they are?" asked Young Puppy.

"*Ani-Quanuhgi*, I think," said 'Squani. "I'm not certain."

"What should we do?"

"For now, just wait and see."

In a short while the men at the edge of the trees began
to move about, to talk to one another, occasionally pointing toward 'Squani and Young Puppy.

"They're wondering who we are and why we're just sitting here," said 'Squani.

"And trying to decide what to do about us," Young Puppy added.

"Yes," said 'Squani. "Just stay as you are. I'm going to try to talk to them."

He urged his mount forward, but just a little. He did not want to give them an easy bow shot, if that was their intention. Then he raised his right arm above his head.

" '*Siyo,*" he called out. "Do any of you speak the language of the Real People?"

He saw some of the men confer briefly with one another. Then one of them stepped out and shouted at him in a strange-sounding language that he did not understand. He tried again, but the second time he used the trade language. Still he was answered in words that held no meaning for him. He tried Spanish with the same results. He looked back over his shoulder at Young Puppy.

"These people," he said, "have no one among them who can speak anything but their own language."

"Look out," said Young Puppy.

'Squani looked back toward the woods just in time to see an arrow fly in his direction. The arrow flew high and far enough for 'Squani and Young Puppy to watch it. It landed a short distance away from 'Squani to his right. He backed his mount until he was once again just beside Young Puppy. He glanced over at the arrow sticking in the ground.

"They're not friendly," he said.

"No," said Young Puppy. "They're not. So. What shall we do?"

"Let's just wait a little longer," said 'Squani. "Let them grow impatient."

They did not have to wait much longer. The leader of the eight men at the tree line suddenly gave out a mighty yell, and, brandishing war clubs, all eight rushed forward at once. Young Puppy glanced nervously toward 'Squani.

"Let them get about halfway to us," said 'Squani, "well away from the trees. Then run your *sogwili* toward them as fast as you can make him go."

'Squani sat still, seeming calm, while Young Puppy grew more and more nervous. One of the attackers flung his war club while running. It came close to Young Puppy, but not close enough to be a serious threat. He held his ground. When the runners hit the halfway mark, 'Squani said, "Now."

He and Young Puppy kicked their mounts almost simultaneously, and both animals leaped forward at once. 'Squani was the first to let out the loud imitation of the turkey gobble, the war cry of the Real People, but he was joined quickly by Young Puppy.

Like their attackers, Young Puppy waved a war club over his head, but 'Squani pulled out his Spanish sword, and as he held it up, the sun glinted off its wide blade.

At first the attackers seemed undaunted, but as the running horses came closer to them, they began to waver. Some of them turned and ran to the sides. The four directly in front of the big animals stopped and braced themselves, but just as they thought they were in danger of being run over, two of them turned and ran. Of the two remaining, one raised his war club and waited for Young Puppy, the other for 'Squani.

"Ride to his right," called 'Squani. The two mounted

warriors aimed their horses so that they would meet their respective opponents right arm to right arm. Again, Young Puppy's mount proved to be the faster of the two. As he came up beside his man, the other was already swinging his club. Young Puppy swung his own in a downward motion, and the handles of the two clubs collided with a loud crack. As Young Puppy rode on past his opponent, he realized that the handle of his club was broken. He tossed the useless weapon aside as he turned his mount.

By then, 'Squani had come up beside the other man. He swung his sword, not at the man's club, but lower, and the steel blade sliced arm muscle. The man screamed and dropped his club. His bleeding arm dangled uselessly at his side. Like Young Puppy, Asquani rode on through the battle line, slowed his mount and turned it, then headed right back.

Young Puppy rode directly toward his enemy. The man took a swing at the beast. It dodged, and he swung again. Frightened, the *sogwili* reared, and the man saw hooves waving in front of his face. He staggered and fell onto his back. Young Puppy jumped from the back of his horse while pulling out his knife. He was on top of the man before the other could get up off his back. With his left hand, Young Puppy grabbed his opponent's right wrist, taking the war club out of play. He raised his own right hand, which clutched the knife, but the man reached up to grab Young Puppy's right wrist with his left hand.

'Squani had no such struggle. His opponent stood helpless, and 'Squani, on his second attack, swung the sword one more time, cutting deeply into the man's neck and killing him instantly.

He looked quickly over at Young Puppy and saw that he

was at least holding his own with the other man. He looked to their right and saw only one of the men who had run from them still out in the open. The others, he guessed, had run back for the safety of the trees. He looked to their left and saw three men. He kicked his horse and raced toward them, and they ran for the trees. He turned and rode past Young Puppy, still struggling with the other man on the ground, and headed for the lone holdout.

When the man saw him coming, he, like the others, ran toward the trees. This time, 'Squani kept riding. He gained quickly on the man afoot and cut him down with one stroke of the Spanish blade as he rode up beside him.

Young Puppy got a knee on the right arm of the other man to hold it down. Then, with his freed left arm, he wrenched the man's fingers from around his wrist and plunged his knife into the man's throat. As the life left the body he straddled, he jumped up and looked around for others to fight, but he saw none. He saw only 'Squani riding back toward him.

"We got three of them," said 'Squani as he rode past Young Puppy at a leisurely pace.

"Then five got away," Young Puppy called out.

'Squani rode on to catch Young Puppy's loose mount by the reins and lead it back to where his companion waited.

"Five ran away," he said, "like cowards." He handed the reins to Young Puppy.

"I have no war club now," said Young Puppy.

"You did well enough without it," said 'Squani, looking at the body there on the ground.

Young Puppy smiled and shrugged.

"Well," he said. "Yes. I guess I did."

'Squani nodded toward the weapon lying in the prairie grass beside the dead man's hand.

"He won't need that one anymore," he said.

Young Puppy gave the war club a doubtful look.

"I don't know," he said. "I don't like to use another man's weapon."

"It's a strong one," said 'Squani. "It broke your own. Besides, you won it. You killed its owner, so now it's yours."

"Well, I guess you're right."

Young Puppy stepped over to pick up the war club. He looked at it and hefted it. Then he smiled.

"It is a good one," he said. "I'll take it."

He swung back up into the saddle and looked at 'Squani.

"Will we chase those other five men?" he asked.

"No. I don't think so," said 'Squani. "They've gone back into the trees. In there, they'd have the advantage over us. The trees are thick on each side of the road there."

"Isn't that the way we were going?"

"Yes, but now, I think, we'd better find another way. Those five will tell their people, and they'll all be wanting to kill us now."

He turned in the saddle and looked off to his right. He could see no change in the basic lay of the land. The prairie stretched on, and so did the edge of the thick forest.

"What are we going to do?" asked Young Puppy.

'Squani turned to look toward the west. Not too far away, the mountains rose. He had lived all his life in the mountains, and so had Young Puppy. If they were to run into any more trouble, he thought, they'd be better off there. Somewhere along the way, if the going got too tough, they might have to abandon the *sogwilis*, but that would be all right. They had started this journey without them, and they could finish it that way if need be. He pointed to the distant mountains.

"I think we should go that way," he said.

Eight

YOUNG PUPPY was elated as they rode across the prairie toward the mountains. He had killed his first enemy in battle. He had not yet killed a Senika to balance things out for his dead brother, but he had definitely proved himself a man. He felt strong, and he felt more confident that he would do what he had sworn to do when at last he reached the Senika country. He was anxious to get there, get it done and get back home. He had visions of returning home to the high praise of his parents, his clan and the whole town of Stikoyi—even neighboring towns of other Real People.

He wanted to yell out in triumph and to ride as fast as the wind. His heart was pounding, and he imagined that he could feel the blood coursing through his veins. He had to fight to control himself, riding along beside the seemingly calm Asquani. It took some time for him to begin to compose himself after the heat of battle and the thrill of victory. He wondered if one day he would be able to do these things as calmly and as casually as Asquan'.

They rode across the prairie and into the mountains to the west. Then they turned north again. They managed to find mountain trails the horses could travel on, although now and then they had to dismount and lead the animals. They knew that there was a possibility that the surviving *Ani-Quanuhgi*, if indeed that's who they had been, might have been spying on them as they made their way toward the mountains, so they were especially watchful for the next few days.

They saw no one though. Because of the speed of the *sogwilis*, thought Asquani, they had traveled farther faster than the *Ani-Quanuhgi* imagined they could. He was confident that, with the time that had passed, there would be no serious pursuit.

It was even likely, he thought, that the *Ani-Quanuhgi* did not know who had killed the three men. They would not have expected to see any Real People riding on the backs of horses or armed with Spanish swords. The only way they would find out who to blame would be if they were lucky enough to spot them again, mounted and armed with the same weapons. There would not likely be any reprisals against the Real People for that unplanned battle. There would not be any reprisals at all, for the *Ani-Quanuhgi* would not know whom or where to strike.

At the end of a long day of riding, they camped in the mountains, and 'Squani, feeling relatively safe and secure, gave Young Puppy the last of the symbols for the writing of the language. He was pleased that the young man had absorbed them all so well. Each time they had camped, he had given just a few more.

Now that Young Puppy had learned them all, 'Squani could give him words to write down. Soon Young Puppy would be comfortable with the writing, and he would be able to write down anything he could say. 'Squani was pleased, but he did find that he was starting to worry even more about the safety of Young Puppy than he had before. He was worrying about the future of the writing.

The next morning they rode down into a pleasant green valley. It was cooler in the valley than it had been on higher ground, and the grass was green and damp. A clear stream ran through the lush valley. Trees lined the stream, and a few trees and shrubs were scattered around the valley floor. More trees surrounded the valley where it rose again into the mountains. They rode to the edge of the stream and dismounted, allowing the animals to drink.

"I think that we're in the country of the *Ani-Senika* now," said 'Squani, his voice soft as if he were afraid he might be overheard.

Young Puppy's heart jumped in his chest, but he said nothing in reply. Instead he looked around. Did he expect to see a Senika so soon, just because of 'Squani's words?

"We'll look for a town, or watch for lone hunters out away from town," 'Squani continued. "I think we should leave our *sogwilis* here so that we'll not be so easily seen."

"Will they still be here when we come back?" asked Young Puppy.

'Squani shrugged.

"I don't know," he said. "This is a good place for them. Maybe they'll stay. But if they wander away, we won't have lost anything. We left home without them. We can go back the same way if we must. While we've had them to ride, our trip was faster and easier."

"It was good of the white man, your friend, to give them to us," said Young Puppy.

"Yes," said 'Squani.

"I'm glad I've learned to ride. And the writing too. 'Squani, I'm glad to have made this journey in your company."

They took a short rest, then turned the two animals loose, stashing the saddles and other tack in the brush that grew along the bank of the stream. Then they walked out of the valley and back up into the mountains. It was two more days before they found a town.

They lay about on the mountainside for the next two days watching, until Asquani was sure that the town was, indeed, Senika, and until they had some familiarity with the comings and goings from the town.

Young Puppy thought that the Senika town seemed much bigger than his own home of Stikoyi, but then he decided that maybe it wasn't really bigger at all. The long houses in the town were bigger than the houses of the Real People. Maybe that just made the town seem bigger.

The first people to come out of the town in a group small enough for the two companions to consider attacking were women and children, and they had agreed already that they would fight and kill only warriors. They hid themselves and let the women and children go about their business and return to the town unmolested. One man came out alone, but he went in the wrong direction. There would have been no sense in going down from the mountain and chasing the man. They waited.

On the fourth day, a man came out of town walking in their direction. He was alone, and he walked out of the town and over to the base of the mountain, just below where the two waited. Then he started to climb. They lost sight of him for a while, but then, as he came closer, they heard him, and then again they could see him.

'Squani nodded to Young Puppy, indicating that the man was his. Then he put his hand on Young Puppy's bow. Young Puppy took the bow in his left hand and nocked an arrow. He waited.

He was crouched behind a boulder, and in order to see his intended victim without exposing himself, he had to peek carefully around the side. Suddenly the man seemed to loom up there before him. Young Puppy stood quickly, drawing back the bowstring as he stood. The man looked up and saw him. His eyes opened wide with surprise. He opened his mouth as if to speak.

"Ah—"

He was unable to say any more. Young Puppy's arrow drove itself deep into the Senika man's chest. He stood and swayed for a moment, looking down at the offending missile. Then he fell forward. Young Puppy had balanced out the death of his brother.

At Asquani's urging, he and Young Puppy then moved farther up the mountain. They selected a spot from which they could view both the town below and the general area where they had left the body. The place was steep, but there were boulders behind which they could hide and rest themselves in relative comfort.

"Sometime someone will come out to look for that man you killed," 'Squani said to Young Puppy. "When they do, we'll see them, and we'll be ready for them."

It was the afternoon of the next day when the buzzards began circling over the side of the mountain. Two heavily armed men came out of the town. Talking, they pointed toward the big birds in the sky. Then they headed for the mountain. They looked all around themselves as they moved.

"They're expecting trouble," 'Squani said.

The two men followed almost the exact path of the man Young Puppy had killed. They might have known where the man had been going. They might only have been judging from the flight of the birds. Perhaps they were only taking the easiest and most common way up the side of the mountain.

Young Puppy tensed. His hand went to the war club at his side. 'Squani put a hand on Young Puppy's arm to stop him.

"Let's use our bows," he said. "We won't have to move from this spot."

It was almost the same as with the one before. They had longer bow shots to make than Young Puppy had made with the other one, but the tactic was the same. They waited. When the men found the body, the two Real People stood up and released their arrows. Young Puppy's arrow hit its mark, and his Senika victim fell forward, dead by the time he hit the ground. 'Squani's arrow struck his target in the right shoulder.

The man howled in pain, surprise and anger, and reached for the arrow with his left hand. He tugged at it, gave up and broke it off. Then he turned to run down the mountainside, but he stumbled and fell. 'Squani was running down toward him, Spanish sword in hand, and Young Puppy was not far behind.

The Senika man rolled over a few times, then struggled back to his feet, just as 'Squani came up behind him.

'Squani swung hard, and the blade bit deep into the side of the man's neck, cutting at an angle on down into the chest. The man was dead before he fell. Young Puppy ran to 'Squani's side.

"*Elikwa,*" said 'Squani. "Let's go home."

"*Howa,*" said Young Puppy. "I'm ready to go. Besides, it's starting to get cold."

There was no pursuit, at least none that ever came near enough for them to be aware of. Even so, they kept watching behind to be sure. They made good time, even traveling on foot in the mountains, and when they arrived back at the green valley, they were surprised to find the two horses still grazing contentedly alongside the little stream. They caught the animals with little trouble and saddled them for the trip back home. They saw no *Ani-Quanuhgi* on their way.

In fact, the entire return trip was uneventful. Young Puppy even thought that it was somewhat boring. Asquani made use of their evenings to reinforce Young Puppy's knowledge of the writing. They managed without too much trouble to avoid towns and other travelers until they were safely back in the land of their own people.

They came to Kituwah first, and their entrance into the town was spectacular, mounted as they were. They told their tale, and they were hailed as returning heroes. There was no longer any doubt as to the status of Young Puppy. He was a young man and a warrior.

Soon, he thought, he would have a new name. He was anxious to get on to his own town of Stikoyi and see what sort of welcome he would receive. But of course, he could not leave Kituwah as long as the people there were feasting and celebrating his feats.

The night was a bit cooler than the hot day, but not so pleasant as the nights had been in the north. The people built a large fire in the ceremonial ground there in front of the townhouse, and they danced and sang almost throughout the night. 'Squani told the tale of their exploits on the trip, and Young Puppy was surprised to hear his friend bragging about him. Young Puppy did not have to tell about his own deeds. 'Squani did it for him.

And Young Puppy was pleasantly surprised also to find the eyes of pretty young women looking his way. He had never before in his young life had that kind of attention from the girls, and he enjoyed it. He felt very much like a man.

In the morning he slept late, like the others, and when he woke up, there were plenty of people in Kituwah ready to feed him. When he was not eating, and it was still early in the day, so the dancing had not begun again, he sat around the council house with the other men and smoked and talked. He thought this trip he made with Asquani had been the best thing he had ever done in his whole life.

And then he began to feel guilty, for he realized that none of this would have happened had it not been for the death of his brother. He loved his brother, and he missed him, yet he could not help but enjoy the praise and attention he was getting. Did that mean he was glad for the death of his brother? He didn't want to think so.

He knew that, when this was all done, they would have the same kind of celebration in Stikoyi when he arrived back home. He hoped that the excitement would have worn off by then. He hoped that he would be able to go through it in a more casual way. He was afraid that if he enjoyed himself as much at home as he was in Kituwah, his mother would notice it for sure. He did not want her to know that he was feeling so good as a result of the killing of Awi-ekwa.

Nine

OSA WAS OVERJOYED to have Asquani safely home. She had tried to endure his absence bravely, but it had all been an act. She had been worried. She wanted her baby to have a father, and she wanted her husband at home with her. She felt as if she really had no home without Asquani. Secretly, she hoped that he would never again go off on such a mission.

Of course, she was proud of him. Celebrations were being held in honor of both him and Young Puppy of Stikoyi, but in Kituwah, 'Squani's home, naturally 'Squani got most of the attention. He was also the older and more experienced of the two men, and therefore he received most of the credit for the success of the raid.

On the other hand, when 'Squani spoke in public, he was quick to give proper credit to Young Puppy and to emphasize the actions of his younger companion. And Young Puppy felt no jealousy. He did not feel slighted. He had never had any attention like this before in his life, so he basked in the shining praise of his deeds of valor. He savored his first taste of glory.

He had also begun, discreetly, he thought, watching a certain beautiful young woman who, he fancied, had been watching him with admiration. Among the Real People, there was no shame or disgrace associated with youthful pursuits of the pleasures of the flesh. It was considered normal behavior and was expected of the young, as long as it was not incestuous or adulterous, and as long as both parties were equally desirous of the activity.

But watching this young woman, Young Puppy found that his thoughts had gone beyond that imagined delight. He found himself thinking that now that he had killed a big deer and had killed three enemies of the Real People, now that he was receiving public recognition as a man and a warrior, now that he had traveled to the north, to the land of the Senikas, and had his own *sogwili* and could ride it, he should be ready to marry.

He had never spoken to this young woman and did not even know her name, but already he was thinking of her as his future wife, and he was hoping that this sudden new dream would be fulfilled in the near future.

During a lull in the festivities, he sought out Asquani, and found him at the *gatayusti* playing field near the townhouse. 'Squani was with a group of men, talking, laughing and placing bets on the outcome of the game. Two men were in the field with their stones and spears.

'Squani saw Young Puppy approach, and he reached out to take his new friend by the hand.

" *'Siyo*," he said.

" *'Siyo*, 'Squan'," said Young Puppy. "Do you have a bet on this game?"

"Yes. I do."

Just then one of the players hurled his disc-like stone and immediately ran after it, raising his spear over his shoulder at the same time. Then he hurled the spear after the stone and stopped to watch. For a long moment, the stone continued to roll and the spear flew through the air with a high trajectory. The stone slowed and wobbled. The spear fell, stabbing its sharp end into the ground. Then the stone fell over on its side, and a great cheer went up from the clusters of men who were standing around. The stone was actually touching the spear. It was a perfect throw.

'Squani threw out his arms in a gesture of resignation.

"Ah well," he said. "I've lost."

"Oh," said Young Puppy, "that's too bad."

"No," said 'Squani. "Anyone who would bet against a man who can throw like that should lose."

"It was an amazing throw," said Young Puppy. He hesitated a moment before continuing. "Will they play again?" he asked.

"Yes," said 'Squani. "I think so."

"Will you bet again?"

"I think not. I've lost enough for one day. Is there something you want?"

"I'd like to talk to you," said Young Puppy, and 'Squani noticed that the young man's face was wearing a very serious expression. He put his arm around his friend's shoulder.

"Let's walk," he said.

They moved away from the crowd and walked past the door to the townhouse. A man coming from the other direction stopped them and engaged them in small talk.

Young Puppy was frustrated. He had important business to discuss with 'Squani, but he remained polite. At last they were able to break away from the chat without seeming to be rude. They walked on for another moment in silence.

"Let's go this way," said Young Puppy, and he turned down a side path that would lead them past some houses, that would, in fact, lead them to the house of 'Squani's wife Osa if they kept going far enough. 'Squani wondered what was troubling Young Puppy, but he didn't ask. The young man would tell him in his own time.

There were people outside in front of their homes, some engaged in various household tasks, some just sitting enjoying the day, and they spoke to the two men as they walked by. Everyone was friendly. The whole town was in a festive mood. Then Young Puppy saw her. She was standing beside a house pounding something, probably hickory nuts, Young Puppy thought, in a *kanona* with a long pole. He thought that he could feel his heart leap in his chest. She looked up and smiled.

" *'Siyo*, 'Squani," she said.

" *'Siyo*. Are you all right today?"

"Yes," she answered.

They kept walking, and Young Puppy struggled with his urge to look back at her. When they had gone on a little farther, he spoke to 'Squani in a low voice.

"What is her name?" he asked.

"Who?"

"The girl you spoke to back there," said Young Puppy. "The one at the *kanona*."

"Oh. That was Guwisti," said 'Squani.

"What's her clan?"

Young Puppy had almost been afraid to ask that question, but it was of vital importance. Should she belong to the Long Hair People, his own clan, he would have to try to drive all thoughts of her from his mind, for she would be a relative and any involvement with her would be incestuous.

"*Ani-Tsisqua*," said 'Squani. "All of these houses along here belong to the Bird People, the people who adopted my wife."

"Is she spoken for?" Young Puppy asked, no longer able to hide his excitement. Then 'Squani realized what was going on in the young man's mind, and he stopped walking and turned to face Young Puppy with a smile.

"No," he said. "I don't think so."

Young Puppy looked at the ground for a brief moment. Then suddenly he reached up, taking 'Squani by both of his shoulders, and looked intently into 'Squani's face.

" 'Squani," he said, "I love Guwisti, and I want to marry her."

"Well," said 'Squani, "she's a lovely young woman. How does she feel about this idea?"

"I don't know. I've never spoken to her."

"If you want to marry her, you should speak to her about it and find out how she feels."

"I've never spoken to her at all."

"Oh, I see," said 'Squani. "Well then. Let's take care of that."

He turned and started to walk back the way they had come, but Young Puppy grabbed him and stopped him.

"Where are you going?" he demanded.

"We're going back to talk to her."

"No," said Young Puppy. "I can't talk to her about that. Not yet."

"Stop worrying. We won't talk about that. It's not my place anyway. After you find out if she's interested, it will be between your mother and her mother. It's a matter for the clans. But we can stop and chat with her, and then the next time you see her, you'll be acquainted already, and you'll be able to talk to her. Come on now. Let's go."

They walked back to the house of Guwisti's mother. They did not walk straight to the house as if they had been deliberately going there. They walked casually, as they had when they passed it initially. Guwisti was still working at the *kanona*. When they were about even with the house, still in the road, she spoke first.

"Hello again," she said. "You just went the other way."

"Yes," said 'Squani. "We're just strolling around. We had something to talk about, but we're through now. Is your father here?"

"No," she said. "I think he went to bet on the *gatayusti* games."

"Oh, that's right," said 'Squani. "I saw him over there. I remember now. I hope he's doing better in the betting than I did."

He started walking off the path and up toward where she stood.

"Do you know my friend here?" he asked. "This is Young Puppy of the Long Hair People, from Stikoyi."

"Of course I know who he is," said Guwisti. "Everyone in town does. There's been much talk about both of you the last two days. Sit down. I'll be right back."

She put down the pounding pole and went into the house as the two men made themselves comfortable on a split log bench in front of the house. She came back out with a bowl in each hand and offered the bowls to her visitors.

"*Wado,*" said 'Squani, and he lifted the bowl to his lips to drink.

"Yes, thank you," said Young Puppy, glad at last to have something to say. He too drank. "This is good *kanohena,*" he said.

"My mother made it," said Guwisti, "but I can make it the same way she does."

Young Puppy took another drink of the thick hominy brew, wishing he could think of something else to say.

"How is your mother?" asked 'Squani.

"She's well," said Guwisti. "Just now she's gone to get some water. She'll be back soon, I think."

"Do you have brothers and sisters?" asked Young Puppy.

"Yes," she said, "but my sisters are all married. They have their own homes now. They're older than me. I have two younger brothers though. They're off somewhere playing like they're men."

'Squani laughed.

"Yes," he said. "That's the way boys are. But your brothers still have a few years left to be boys."

Guwisti laughed just a little, and Young Puppy thought that her laughter sounded like the song of a bird. She was wonderful, he thought. His whole body and his soul ached for her. How long, he wondered, would it be before he would be able to bring himself to speak his feelings to her? He did not know if he would be able to stand it. And what if, while he was waiting for the right time, someone else spoke to her first? Ah, if that should happen, he thought, he would die.

'Squani turned up his bowl and finished off the *ka-nohena*. Then he stood up. Young Puppy saw what was happening and quickly drained his bowl.

"I guess we'll go now," said 'Squani. "Maybe I'll find your father still at the games."

Guwisti laughed again, and the aches in the body and soul of Young Puppy throbbed and tortured him.

"Probably he's still there," she said.

'Squani started to walk away. Young Puppy followed him for two steps, then hesitated and turned around to face Guwisti.

"I enjoyed the visit," he said.

"Thank you," said Guwisti. "I did too. Come again to see me."

His heart danced inside his chest, and in spite of himself, he smiled broadly.

"Yes," he said. "Thank you. I will."

He had never felt so strange in all his life. He was happy, almost deliriously so. He had actually met her and talked with her. He knew her name and her clan and where she lived. She had given him *kanohena*, and she had spoken to him and smiled at him. And best of all, she had actually invited him to come back. She had encouraged him.

Yet he still ached for her, and he was impatient to find a way to ease the pain. And there was still the fear that someone else would come along and speak before he could. There was also the chance that their families would not agree, or that the conjurer, whoever her mother might consult, would not perceive it to be a proper match. Any number of things could go wrong, and they were all unpleasant to contemplate.

Well, the festivities would continue for two more days, so he would stay in Kituwah until they were done. Then he would have to go on to Stikoyi. He would have to see his own parents and his own clanspeople and townspeople. They would have heard by now of the success of the mission, and they would be anxious to put on their own celebration.

He thought all this through. He would have to act quickly. He would have to find a way to see Guwisti alone. He would have to tell her how he felt. And he would have to accomplish all this in the next two days. He was determined. He would do it. And he was confident. After all, she had encouraged him.

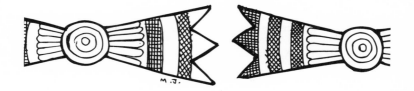

Ten

I T WAS THE MORNING of the third day of the celebration in Kituwah. Nothing much was going on, for
the dancing from the day before had lasted well into the
night. Most people had gotten up and gone down to the
river to start the day, as they should, but many of them had
gone back home to bed. Some, coming out of the water,
just found the nearest comfortable spot, under a tree,
against the front wall of a house, anywhere they could rest
or sleep. A few sat around in small groups talking about
the festivities and laughing. Here and there a woman could
be seen actually at work.

Just outside the walls of Kituwah a cluster of men stood
studying the two *sogwilis* that 'Squani and Young Puppy
had brought back with them from their adventure. For
some, it was the first time they had ever seen such an animal. Others had seen them, but rarely. The animals, with
trailing reins, were grazing contentedly.

"So they're not just to carry things on their backs," said one. "They're for riding on as well."

"Apparently," said another. "Asquani and Young Puppy came back home from the Senika country riding on their backs."

"And they have those *gayahulos*, those special seats which they wear on their backs," said another, "for the riders to sit on."

"They look something like deer or big deer, but they have no antlers. I wonder if they're good to eat."

"They might be, but it would be a waste to eat them when there are so few of them, and they're useful for other things."

"Yes. You're right about that, I think. Look, here comes Asquani."

'Squani joined the group, and they continued to talk about the horses. They asked questions and he answered them, and as they talked, 'Squani moved closer to one of the grazing animals. As he continued to answer their questions, he stroked the horse's neck and patted it on the rump. Soon others moved up close enough to touch the animal.

Others came out the gateway to join the group—men, women and children. Among them were Osa and Guwisti. A little later another bunch came out. Carrier and Potmaker were with them, leading their little son, Asquani's young half brother. Even Young Puppy came strolling out to see what was going on. Most of the inhabitants of Kituwah who were awake, it seemed, were there outside the wall.

The crowd was mostly pressed around Asquani and the one horse. The second animal grazed alone and was mostly ignored. No one wanted to approach it alone, without its owner there.

Then Young Puppy saw Guwisti in the crowd, and he decided that he must get some of the attention away from Asquani and his *sogwil'*. He thought a moment, and then he walked over to the outside of the town wall where the two saddles lay. He picked up one saddle and carried it to the as yet undisturbed horse. He put the saddle on the ground and took the head of the *sogwili* in his hands and spoke to it in a low voice. He pretended not to notice when a few of the people began moving in his direction.

Then he threw a small blanket on the animal's back and on top of that, the saddle—the *gayahulo*, as the others had begun to call it. The people watched, fascinated, as he fastened and tightened a number of straps. And then he heard his name spoken by a lovely, musical voice.

"Young Puppy," said Guwisti, "are you going to ride it?"

He turned toward her, and she stood there in the crowd, a vision of loveliness. He shrugged, trying hard to appear nonchalant.

"Yes," he said, "I think she needs to run a little."

He climbed up onto the animal's back and settled into the saddle. He looked down on the crowd gathered there and saw the wonder on their faces, and his chest seemed to swell with pride. He glanced at Guwisti where she stood, and he imagined that he saw in her look a special kind of interest. He gave a flick of the reins and a slight kick with his heels.

"Ha," he said, and the *sogwili* started to trot. People stepped back, afraid that it might run in their direction, step on them or knock them over, and their voices expressed amazement. The crowd around Asquani had gotten smaller.

"Will you ride this one?" a man asked him.

Asquani smiled in the direction of Young Puppy.

"Yes," he said, "perhaps I should."

"I'll get the *gayahulo* for you," said the man, and he ran toward the wall. Soon Asquani, too, was riding. The two men rode out away from the town, and then they turned and rode back. They rode around the crowd of observers. They walked, they trotted and they raced. Young Puppy stopped close to the crowd, right in front of Guwisti. He looked down at her. He felt bold, and, he thought, there may never be another opportunity like this one.

"Would you like to ride?" he said. He astonished himself with his boldness, but then, he didn't feel like himself. He felt like someone else. He didn't know who, but not Young Puppy.

"I don't know how," she said.

"Come on," he said, holding out his hand toward her. "Ride with me. I'll show you how."

He dismounted and helped her into the saddle. Then he jumped on behind. He reached around her to hold the reins, and her closeness sent a thrill unlike any he had ever known through his entire body. He struggled to maintain his poise.

He walked the horse, showing Guwisti the use of the reins. Then he kicked it into a trot. Soon he gave her the reins, and a little later, he slid off the backside and let her handle the horse all by herself. She did well for her first try, and in a little while, she rode back and stopped there where he waited.

"It's fun," she said.

"Can I ride it?" called out a voice from the crowd. Soon they were all taking turns riding the horses, with instructions from both Young Puppy and Asquani, but Guwisti got more than her share of turns. Some people noticed, and they started to talk.

"Look. Young Puppy is favoring Guwisti."

"He likes her."

"I think she likes him too."

"Maybe. Maybe she just wants to ride his *sogwili*."

"Do her parents know?"

"How could they not know? They're standing just over there."

Someone was riding Asquani's horse, and Osa stood by her husband's side.

"People are talking about your young friend," she said.

"What are they saying?" he asked her.

"You really haven't noticed?"

"No."

"They're saying that he's interested in Guwist'."

'Squani smiled and put his arm around her shoulders.

"They're right, of course," he said. "He wants to marry her."

When the dancing and singing in Kituwah were done, and Young Puppy was back home in Stikoyi, there was another four-day celebration in his honor, and this time he was the center of attention. He was pleased with this, of course, but it all seemed a bit anticlimactic to him. He had been honored for four days in Kituwah along with Asquani. He had thought that he would be more excited to have the same thing happening in his own town with his parents and all of his friends there. And he was, to some extent. He was not ungrateful, but somehow it was not what he had expected. For a while he wondered what was wrong with him, but then he knew.

It was Guwisti, of course. His heart could not be in the celebration at Stikoyi when Guwisti was back in Kituwah. Then he realized that Stikoyi would no longer be his home. When he married Guwisti, he would go live with her, in her house, in Kituwah. He wanted her so badly, he thought, that already in his heart Kituwah was his new home. He had to tell his mother.

The morning of the second day, he was awake early, even though they had danced late into the night. His father and mother and little sister were all still asleep. He was impatient for his mother to wake up. The other two could sleep all day for all he cared, or at least until it was time for the dancing again that night. But he wanted his mother to wake up.

Impatient, he dressed himself and went to the river's edge. There he undressed and waded into the cold water. He made a special prayer that morning as he ducked under the surface. He got out, shivered violently once and sat down in a patch of early morning sun, and realized that the days were getting colder. Little bumps popped out all over his wet skin in spite of the warm sun. A cool breeze was blowing.

Mostly dried, he dressed himself again and walked back to his mother's house. As he stepped inside, she stirred. He decided that she was awake, and he whispered to her.

"*Etsi.*"

She stirred again and moaned.

"*Etsi*," he said, still in a whisper. He did not want to wake the others. "*Etsi*. Are you awake?"

Lolo raised her head a little and looked at him through squinted eyes.

"I'm awake now, I guess," she said.

"I need to talk to you," he said. "It's something very important."

"All right," she said. "I'll be up right away."

Her husband rolled over onto his back and groaned.

"What is it?" he asked.

"*Hla gohusdi*, Yona-hawiya," she said. "It's nothing. Go back to sleep."

Taking her at her word, Bear Meat rolled back over onto his left side with another groan and pulled the cover up to his chin.

"I'll be outside," Young Puppy whispered, and he ducked to go through the door. Impatient, he paced in front of the house until Lolo at last emerged. Still rubbing her eyes, she felt the cool morning breeze and noticed right away that her son wore no shirt and his long hair was wet.

"You've been to the river," she said.

"Of course," he said.

"You should have a shirt on," she said, and she went back inside. A moment later she came out again, and she handed her son one of his buckskin shirts. He took it and pulled it on over his head.

"I should go to the river," she said.

"They're all out by now," said Young Puppy.

"So? I can go in by myself."

"Yes. Well. Are you going then?"

"Yes," she said.

"I'll walk along with you."

By the time they had reached the bank of the river, Young Puppy had told his mother all about Guwisti. He told her what she looked like, what she sounded like, where she lived, what clan she belonged to and the names of her parents. He even told her how well Guwisti had managed to ride his horse the first time she had tried it alone.

"*Etsi,*" he said, "I want her to be my wife."

"I would think so," she said, a slight edge of sarcasm in her tone, "if she is so perfect as you say. Can she walk on water too and fly in the air?"

"*Etsi,*" said Young Puppy, "I'm serious about this matter."

They had stopped beside the river, and Lolo looked at her son for a long moment.

"You're sure about this girl?" she said. "You really want to marry?"

"Yes."

"Well then, we can't do anything until this celebration is done," she said, "but when it's over, I'll go to Kituwah and talk to her mother. Diguhsgi, you say. Of the Bird People?"

"Yes."

"*Howa.* You run along now. I'm going in the water."

"Yes," he said, and his smile was so big that it seemed like it would tear his face apart. He almost danced with joy. He put his hands on his mother's shoulders and then took them away as he danced back. "Yes. Of course. Thank you, Mother. Thank you."

Then he turned and ran back toward the main part of

the town. His spirit soared above him. The world was a more beautiful place than he had ever noticed it to be before. His life was wonderful, for he was the most fortunate of men among the Real People, the greatest people in the world. Guwisti was going to be his wife.

Eleven

LOLO TOOK her whole family with her to Kituwah. She sat on the back of the *sogwili* while Young Puppy led it along by the reins. She sat tall and straight. She felt puffed up. Not every mother of the Real People had a son who could take her around on the back of a *sogwili*.

Yona-hawiya walked along beside her. Usdi, the little girl, alternately rode behind the saddle or on her father's shoulders. Occasionally, she insisted on being let down to the ground where she walked or ran along.

By the time they reached Kituwah, Usdi was asleep. Yona-hawiya went to the townhouse to see if he could find some men of his own clan with whom to sit and smoke and visit. Lolo, carrying the sleeping Usdi, went with Young Puppy to find the house of Guwisti's mother. He pointed it out to her, and then he left. He walked on down the way looking for Asquani, but instead he found Osa at home alone.

"He's up on the mountain with other Wolves watching the pass," she said.

Young Puppy thanked her and went on his way. He remembered that the first time he had met Asquani, the adopted Wolf Person had been at work guarding the pass. He was disappointed though. He had known that he wouldn't be able to hang around the house of his intended mother-in-law while his mother negotiated with her. He wondered if Guwisti was at home. Would she sit and listen to the talk, or would she leave too? He didn't know.

He headed for the townhouse, not knowing what else to do. Suddenly he saw a young man rushing toward him. It startled him at first, but then the young man spoke.

" *'Siyo*, Young Puppy," he said. *"Tohiju?"*

"Uh, tohigwu," Young Puppy answered. *"Nihina?"*

"I'm doing well too," said the other man. "Do you remember me?"

Young Puppy hesitated. He did not really recall the young man. He had met so many people in Kituwah during the four days of ceremony that he could not possibly remember them all. Still he was embarrassed.

"I'm called Olig'," the man said.

"Yes," said Young Puppy. "Of course."

"I saw you come in. Did you come from Stikoyi today?"

"Yes," said Young Puppy. "With my family."

"You brought your *sogwili*," said Olig'. "Can I ride it?"

Young Puppy did not want to teach riding just then, and he did not want anyone riding his horse without his supervision. Still, he did not want to seem rude or stingy by simply giving a blunt refusal.

"She's had a long ride with someone on her back," he said. "Right now she needs a rest. Maybe after a while."

"Ha," said Olig'. "She looks plenty strong to me."

"She is," said Young Puppy. "She just needs to rest. That's all."

"I'll bet that if Guwisti wanted a ride, you'd go right out there. I'll bet you'd run that big, ugly animal to death for her."

Just then another man stepped up. He had overheard enough of the conversation to know what was going on.

"Olig'," he said, "you're being rude to a guest in our town."

"I only want to ride his *sogwil'*," said Olig'.

Young Puppy looked at the newcomer, glad to have a witness to the proceedings.

"I told him," he said, "that the *sogwil'* is too tired, but he insists." He looked back at Olig'. "Come on then," he said. "I guess she can stand a little more."

The three men walked out of the town together, and as they went, others followed. Soon they had gathered outside the walls where Young Puppy had left his horse and saddle. The saddle was on the ground near the wall.

Young Puppy went to the saddle and squatted down beside it. He looked around until he spotted a small rough rock. Then he picked up the blanket and glanced over toward the horse.

"*Sogwili*," he said. "How are you feeling after your long walk?"

As he spoke to the horse, the others standing around looked at it as if they thought that it might actually answer Young Puppy's question. As they did, Young Puppy picked up the jagged rock. He felt it with his thumb and was delighted to find that it had a good sharp edge. He stood up and walked over to the horse, throwing the blanket up on its back, and he slipped the rock in under the blanket, carefully turning the sharp edge down against the animal's flesh. Then he went back for the saddle.

Carrying the saddle, he walked back to the side of the horse. He stood there a moment, and he looked at Olig'.

"I told you that she's tired," he said. "Are you sure you want to do this?"

"I want to ride the *sogwili*," said Olig'.

Young Puppy swung the saddle up in place and secured all the straps. The people standing there gathered around and watched his every move. At last he stepped back and gestured with one arm toward the waiting animal.

"Go on," he said.

Olig' hurried forward and practically jumped into the saddle. The animal nickered and flinched. It stomped and blew. It turned in a tight circle and fidgeted.

"She doesn't like you on her back," said Young Puppy. "She wants to rest."

"I want to ride," said Olig', and he kicked the horse hard in the sides. She whinnied loud and jumped forward, unsettling the man on her back, but he recovered himself quickly.

"Go," he shouted. "Run, *sogwil'*. Go."

Suddenly she reared, and Olig' almost fell backward out of the saddle. He threw his weight forward just as her front legs came down, and he fell across her neck. Then she kicked back with her hind legs. He slid some to the right, but he held tight around her neck. Then she started to kick and buck in earnest. She wanted the man off her back.

She jumped straight up with all four feet off the ground, and Olig' momentarily left the saddle as they started back down. The horse's feet hit the ground, and then Olig's backside hit the saddle.

"Ah," he shouted.

Then she started to twist and turn, and Olig' started to moan loudly as he felt his weight being slung off to one side. Then she stopped suddenly, turned the other direction, jumped and kicked with her hind legs all at once, and Olig' went flying into the air.

"Ahh," he screamed as he flew. He went high over the horse's head. His arms were outstretched. He saw the ground rushing at him, and in desperation, he ducked his head. That caused him to turn in the air, and he landed hard on his back with a loud, dull thud. A cloud of dust rose around him, as he lay still but gasping for air, the wind knocked from his lungs.

The horse continued to kick and buck, but not as much as before. Young Puppy ran for her head.

"What's wrong with you?" he said. "Calm down. Calm down. It's me. Be still now."

Soon he got hold of the reins, and then he held the animal's head in his hands, and he stroked her and talked to her in a soft voice. She blew and snorted and stamped, but she was settling down. Young Puppy looked over at Olig', still on his back and gasping for his breath.

"What did you do to my *sogwil'*?" he shouted.

Feigning indignant anger, he led her back over beside the wall and removed the saddle and blanket, carefully palming the little rock. He stayed there beside the horse, rubbing her and consoling her.

"You should have listened to Young Puppy," he heard someone say to Olig'. "You might have hurt his *sogwil'*."

Olig', having some breath in his lungs at last, sat up.

"I could have been hurt," he shouted between gasps for air. "That crazy animal threw me hard."

"He told you to leave it alone," someone answered. "You should have listened to him. If you got hurt, it would have been your own fault."

The others all went back inside the walls. Several of them spoke to Young Puppy as they passed him by. Olig' finally hobbled in, still sulking. Soon Young Puppy was alone with his horse. For a while he rubbed her back and patted her flanks. He pressed his head against hers, and he talked to her. Finally he sat down near her head and leaned back against the wall. Soon the animal was again contentedly eating grass.

Young Puppy wondered for a moment if he had done the right thing by humiliating Olig'. He could as easily have let the man ride the horse. But it had been Oliga's attitude and arrogance that had caused Young Puppy to do what he had done. Had the man taken him at his word when he said that the horse was tired, Young Puppy would have let him ride her at a later time.

After thinking it all over, he decided that he had done the right thing. Olig' had needed to be taught a lesson, even a rough one like this. And, after all, there had been no permanent damage done. Olig' had gotten up and walked back inside the wall without any help. No bones had been broken.

But perhaps Young Puppy had made an enemy of Olig'. Well, what of that? He told himself, if the man was that big a fool, so be it. He would be ready to fight Olig' anytime he was ready. He didn't particularly like the thought of having an enemy among the Real People, especially in

Kituwah, where he was planning to make his home, but he had not asked for this trouble. Olig' had.

He heard soft footsteps in the grass to his right, in the direction of the gateway, and he looked. Guwisti was walking toward him. He got quickly to his feet.

" *'Siyo,*" he said.

" *'Siyo.* I heard about what just happened out here," she said.

"Oh, that. Yes, well," he said, looking at the ground. "Is that man very angry at me?"

"Olig'?" she said. "Yes. He is, but everyone is telling him that it was his own fault."

"It was," said Young Puppy. "Sort of."

"Sort of?" she said.

"He's not a relative of yours?"

"No."

"A friend?"

"No. I know him, of course, but—no. He's nothing special to me."

"Oh, good," he said. "Then I'll tell you."

He told her of his meeting with Olig', and how Olig' had insisted on riding the horse even after he had protested. Then he told her about the small rock and how it had caused the horse to buck. She laughed, and he laughed with her. When their laughter subsided, they sat silent for a moment.

"Is my mother still talking with your mother?" he asked her.

"Yes. They were still talking just now when I left to come out here."

He looked at the ground between his feet.

"I hope that my mother agrees," she said.

"You do?" he said, looking up at her.

"Yes."

"Oh," he said. "That makes me very happy."

"Of course, Mother will have to talk to other women in the clan after that, and I guess your mother will have to do the same."

"Yes. I know," he said.

"And then they'll have to go to someone to see if we'll be good together."

"I'm not worried about that," he said. "I know we will."

Now she looked at the ground, and a slight blush lit up her cheeks.

"Yes," she said. "I know we will too."

"Do you want to go for a ride?" Young Puppy asked.

"Has the *sogwili* had enough rest?"

"Oh, she's all right. Come on."

He saddled the horse and helped Guwisti up onto its back. Then he got up behind her. From a perch on a climbing pole behind the wall, Olig' watched as they rode away from town.

They rode for a while just feeling the wind in their faces, feeling the freedom, and then he turned the animal toward the river, where the trees lined the bank, where no one would see them. He slid off the back and wrapped the reins around a small sapling. Then he helped Guwisti down, and they walked into the trees.

They sat beside the clear running water, and they talked. They sat together in silence. They sat closer and closer together until their bodies touched, and he put his arm around her. They pressed together tightly, and she lay back, pulling him toward her, pulling him down on top of her, and his head was swimming in a world of wonders.

Twelve

BACK HOME at Stikoyi, Young Puppy was impatient. His mother was still talking with other women of the Long Hair Clan, and as far as he knew, the talks among the Bird Clan women in Kituwah were continuing. He didn't even know if the two mothers had yet agreed, for his own mother wouldn't tell him anything. Just that they were talking, and that if he should happen to see Diguhsgi again, he should not speak to her. That was encouraging, of course, for it meant that he was to start behaving as if Diguhsgi was his mother-in-law.

"These things take time," she said.

He wished that they could hurry and resolve the situation. What could be their problem? He was a good-looking young man. He was healthy and strong. He had proved himself to be a good hunter and a brave warrior. And on top of all that, Guwisti had made it clear that she wanted him. What more could they want?

More experience? He had gone on the war trail only

once, and then he had been accompanied by an older and more experienced man. He had killed three enemies. Yet at the conclusion of the four-day ceremony in Kituwah and the second four-day ceremony in Stikoyi, no one had given him a new name. He still wore the boy's name of Young Puppy.

He decided that he must need more experience at war, and furthermore, he decided that he must go out on his own the next time. He did not want to be seen as anybody's young puppy on his next foray. He would stand alone.

Then he recalled the number of days it had taken him and Asquani to reach the land of the *Ani-Senika*, accomplish their task and return home. And they had been riding *sogwilis* most of the way. He did not think that he could afford to be away from home that long. Not at this time. Not while the clan women were discussing his future with Guwisti.

He would have to select a closer enemy. It was really no trouble to find enemies nearby. The Real People had been at war off and on with most of their neighbors. The problem was that, though no formal peace had been concluded with, say, the *Ani-Chahta*, there had been no recent trouble between the two peoples. An attack on the *Ani-Chahta*, therefore, would serve to rekindle the old animosities and cause reprisals against towns of the Real People. The same was true of most of the other so-called enemy neighbors.

For two days he thought about this problem. He knew that he would have to do something soon, or the worry would make him crazy. Then it came to him that there were many towns of Real People, and that he did not know what was happening in the more distant towns. If there had been any recent troubles with neighboring enemies that he had not yet heard about, it would likely be at one of the frontier towns farthest from Stikoyi.

He knew less about the towns to the far southwest of the territory of the Real People, and so he decided that he would try there. Turkey Town, he thought. Of course. His mother's oldest brother had married a woman from Turkey Town and moved to her home. It was perfect. The trip would not take so long on the back of his *sogwili*, and he just might find some active warfare being waged out there. He made up his mind.

He didn't want to just ride off without telling anyone. Not at a time when he was under consideration by the women of the Bird Clan as a prospective husband. He would have to tell his mother something to explain his absence, but he did not want to give her his real reason for going. He talked to his mother the next morning before she left her house.

"Etsi," he said, "this waiting around for a decision about my marriage is making me crazy. I think I'll go on a trip for a few days."

"Oh?" she said. "Where will you go?"

"I want to go to Turkey Town to visit my uncle, Gusa-dihi."

He waited for that announcement to settle in and have its full effect on her. Gusa-dihi was his mother's oldest brother, and had he not married a woman from another town too far away for frequent visits, he would have been the uncle to instruct and discipline Young Puppy on his way to manhood. And Lolo had not seen her brother for some time. Young Puppy knew he had hit a soft spot.

"I think that's a good idea," she said. "It won't take you

so long to get there on your *sogwili*, and you should visit with your uncle before you take a wife. Find out how he and his wife and children are doing. Find out all the news you can before you come back home, so you can tell me."

"I will, *Etsi*," said Young Puppy.

"Maybe my brother would even like to accompany you when you come back home," she said.

"I'll ask him."

"And don't stay too long."

"No," he said. "I won't. Only a few days. Maybe when I come back, the decision will have been made."

"Maybe so," she said.

He packed his things and saddled his horse and left that very morning for Turkey Town.

Asquani was scouting. Since the Senika man had gotten through their lines of defense, the Wolf People who guarded the passes decided that they must be more vigilant. They not only kept their usual posts, they began sending out scouts to watch for anyone who might be coming their way. And Asquani had a horse. That meant that he could range out farther, faster, and if he should see anything that might be threatening, he could get back with the news in a hurry.

He was on a high mountain ridge when he saw the six travelers down below. All men. All armed and painted for war. He thought that they were *Ani-Senika*, but he could not be sure. He turned his horse and rode back toward Kituwah, just far enough to get well ahead of the travelers. They were not yet close enough to the town to be worried about being seen, for they were still traveling along the road.

He left his *sogwili* up on the mountain path, and he made his way down the side of the rocky, tree-covered incline. He found a spot from which he would be able to see them, and he waited. Soon they were almost even with him. They were near enough for him to have killed one with a bow shot, but that was not his purpose. He studied them closely as they passed him by, and he heard two of them exchange a few words. It was enough.

He waited for them to get a little farther ahead, and then he climbed back up to where his *sogwili* waited for him. He mounted and rode hard back to the guard post near Kituwah.

"Six *Ani-Senika* are coming," he said.

"How close are they?" asked Trotting Wolf.

"We can still get to them, I think, before they leave the road," said 'Squani, "if we hurry."

"You ride back again," said Trotting Wolf. "If they stay on the road, just wait for us. If they leave the road, come back to let us know. We'll all stay on the mountain trail until we meet."

The plan worked. Asquani, high up on the mountain trail, spotted the Senikas still on the road below. He back-tracked just a little. When Trotting Wolf and the others came along, they had just enough time to move down the mountainside and set up an ambush with men on both sides of the road. If they had not gotten to just this spot, 'Squani figured, they would have been too late. Around the next bend, the Senikas would most likely have left the road and taken to the wooded hillsides themselves. They waited.

Hiadeoni felt as if the deaths of the three men back home were on his own head. The men would probably not have been killed had it not been for his own raid into the country of the Cave People in retaliation for the death of his uncle, Gana. He was not regretful that he had killed the two Cave People, but he did feel enough responsibility that he was compelled to lead a more substantial raid back down south to even the score for the three who had been so recently killed.

Alone he had killed two. Now he had five warriors with him, all good men. He could show them the way he had managed to slip past the guards on his last trip, and the six of them together should be able to inflict substantial losses on the hated Cave People.

"We're in their territory now," he told his companions. "We'll leave the road soon—just around that next curve, I think. By the time the sun is low in the sky, we'll be in the mountains above their town."

"Good," said the man nearest Hiadeoni. "My war club is thirsty for their blood."

Then the air was split by the chilling imitation of the cry of the wild turkey, and men stood up from behind bushes and boulders on both sides of the road. The six Senika men were caught in a deadly cross fire of flying arrows.

The man with the thirsty war club was hit in the temple by an arrow that drove itself all the way through his head. He dropped like a rock. A stone-headed war club flung with mighty force smashed into the right shoulder of Hiadeoni. Helpless, he looked around himself and saw three of his companions fall with arrows in them.

"Run," he shouted. "Save yourselves. Run."

And he himself ran. He ran without looking back. He was running away from the land of the Cave People. He ran, hoping that others were also running. He ran with the throbbing pain in his useless shoulder and arm. He ran until he could no longer hear the shouts of Cave People pursuing him, and then he ran some more. He ran until his lungs felt as if they would burst, and then he staggered off the road to fall over in some tall grass. He lay there gasping for breath.

Back at the site of the ambush, Trotting Wolf stepped out into the road. As he looked at the four bodies, the other guardians of the pass came out to stand with him.

"Two ran away," said 'Squani. "I think they're both hurt. We could probably catch them easily."

"No," said Trotting Wolf. "Let them go. If they're badly hurt, they'll die before they can make it back to their own country. And even if they should make it back alive, that will be all right. They can tell the other *Ani-Senika* what happened to them when they tried to come into the country of the Real People."

"*Howa*," said Asquani. "Maybe any others who might be thinking of coming to visit us will be discouraged by their news."

"Yes," said Trotting Wolf. "But just in case they should come this far in spite of what happened to their friends, let's give them some further discouragement. Let's cut the heads off these four men and set them up on poles along the sides of the road."

It was dark. Hiadeoni had fallen asleep there in the tall grass. He came back to his senses when he heard the sound of footsteps on the road coming toward him. Painfully, he lifted up his head to look and listen, and then he heard the additional sound of heavy breathing. Then he noticed that the sound of the footsteps was strange. There was a heavy step followed by a dragging noise. Slowly, trying not to give away his own position, he sat up.

In the darkness, he could see the shadowy figure of a man coming toward him in the road, and the man was limping badly, dragging one hurt leg behind him. He waited a little longer, trying to see the man more clearly in the dim moonlight, and then he recognized one of his companions.

"Grey Owl," he said. "It is I, Hiadeoni."

"Ah," said Grey Owl. "You frightened me."

"I was frightened too until I recognized you," said Hiadeoni.

With some difficulty, he got himself up and moved out into the road. He stepped just to the right side of Grey Owl so that his good shoulder would be nearest the other wounded man, and he noted that it was Grey Owl's right leg that was dragging.

"Lean on me," he said.

Grey Owl put his right hand on the left shoulder of Hiadeoni.

"Ah," he said, and he forced a small laugh. "We're lucky to be hurt on the same side."

"Yes," said Hiadeoni, and he chuckled through a groan from the pain in his right shoulder. "We'll have to give thanks for that. How bad is your leg?"

"An arrow hit my thigh. I broke it off, but a short piece and the point are still in there. Deep, I think. I think it's near the bone. I know it hurts. What about your shoulder?"

"It's smashed," said Hiadeoni. "Useless. Are there any others of us left?"

"No," said Grey Owl. "The others are all dead. Only we are left alive, and we're not good for anything, I think."

"No," said Hiadeoni. "All we can do is try to get ourselves back home. Are we still being pursued?"

"I don't think so. They killed four. They know they hurt us. They probably don't think that we'll live long in this condition."

"But we will live," said Hiadeoni. "Somehow we'll live, and our wounds will heal, and then we'll come back here again. And the next time we come, things will be very different."

Thirteen

W HEN YOUNG PUPPY rode into Turkey Town, everyone there was astonished to see a young man of the Real People mounted on one of the strange animals they called *sogwilis*. His uncle, Gusa-dihi, saw him, recognized him and looked upon him with pride.

"This is my nephew," he called out to his neighbors. "This is my sister's son. From Stikoyi."

" '*Siyo*, Uncle," said Young Puppy.

"I've never seen anyone ride on a *sogwil'*," said Gusa-dihi, "except for a *'Squan'*."

"It was Asquani who taught me to ride," said Young Puppy.

"What?"

Young Puppy laughed and jumped down from the back of his horse. He told his uncle about his trip to the land of the *Ani-Senika* with the man known as Asquani.

"Have you heard about Asquani?" he asked.

"Oh yes," said Gusa-dihi. "I seem to recall now. Even

way out here, we heard about that man. So. You rode with Asquani all the way up north, and you killed three *Ani-Senika?*"

"No, Uncle," said Young Puppy. "I killed only two *Ani-Senika*. 'Squani killed the other. The third enemy I killed was not a Senika. That was in the fight along the way."

"Oh yes," said Gusa-dihi. "Well, Nephew, I'm proud of you. So tell me, how is my sister?"

"She's well," said Young Puppy.

"Come on," said his uncle. "Come with me to my wife's house. She'll give you something to eat, and then we'll talk."

For the rest of that day and all of the next, they visited, catching each other up on news regarding members of the family and different towns of the Real People. Young Puppy waited for a lull in the conversation, and then he told his uncle about Guwisti. He told him about the discussions that were taking place among the women of the two clans and how the wait was making him crazy.

"Ah," said Gusa-dihi, "when the women start talking, all we can do is wait."

Then Gusa-dihi took his nephew all around Turkey Town, introducing him to everyone and bragging about his recent accomplishments, and Young Puppy taught Gusa-dihi and some others how to ride the horse.

Between the *sogwil'* and his uncle's boasting, Young Puppy quickly became a celebrity in Turkey Town. Everyone wanted to talk to him, and everywhere he went the people fed him. He enjoyed this special attention, but soon he had to remind himself that he had not come to Turkey

Town to be pampered. He had a purpose. And his mother had told him not to stay away too long.

"Uncle," he said.

It was late in the evening, and the two men were sitting outside the house of Gusa-dihi's wife. They were smoking short clay pipes, talking about nothing in particular and enjoying the unusually mild weather so late into the year.

"Yes?"

"Here at Turkey Town," said Young Puppy, "you're so close to the country of the *Ani-Gusa.* Are you safe here from attacks?"

"We have a strong town here," said Gusa-dihi. "Lots of young, strong warriors. And we have men out watching all the time."

"Yes. So do we."

"Um. Anyway, there's only one *Gusa* town very near us, and they won't attack. They know how strong we are."

"Are you at peace with them then?"

"No. Sometimes hunters from here meet up with ones from over there out in the woods, and then they fight. But it's been a long time now since we've attacked their town, and longer since they've dared attack us here."

"How near is this town of *Ani-Gusa?*"

"It's only about a four-day walk from here," said Gusa-dihi, lifting up his arm and pointing to the southwest, "in that direction."

Young Puppy nodded and puffed his pipe. He was trying to get out of his uncle the information he wanted without betraying his reasons for wanting it.

"You said that hunters sometimes meet and fight," he said. "Is there a dispute then about your hunting grounds?"

"Yes," said Gusa-dihi. "There's a river between our land and that of the *Ani-Gusa*, and the area between here and the river has always been ours. On the other side of the river, it belongs to them. Everyone knows that. But recently the *Ani-Gusa* have been crossing the river and hunting in there, and they claim that it belongs to them. That's where most of the fights take place. One of these days we'll have to settle the issue for good. We'll have to have a war with them."

"Is the hunting good in that place you're talking about? Is that why they're coming in there?"

"Ah yes. *Awi, awi-ekwa,* even sometimes *yansa.* The game is plentiful. But it's just as good on their side of the river. Who knows why a *Gusa* does anything? Maybe they want to start a war. I don't know."

Young Puppy puffed at his pipe, but the flame had gone out. He turned it over and tapped it on the side to loosen the dottle and let it drop out on the ground.

"Do the hunting rights to that area belong to just one clan?" he asked.

"No," said Gusa-dihi. "Not in there. Anyone can hunt in there. Anyone of the Real People."

"Well then, if it's all right with you, I think I'll go in there and hunt tomorrow," said Young Puppy.

"Good," said Gusa-dihi. "Of course it's all right. I'll take you."

"No, Uncle," said Young Puppy. "I need to go alone this time."

Gusa-dihi looked at Young Puppy with curiosity, but he said nothing. If the young man felt the need to hunt alone, that was his business. He wouldn't interfere. A few years ago, he might have, on the grounds that Young Puppy needed his instruction, but those years were gone. He had missed them by living in Turkey Town with his wife's people. Now his nephew was a man.

"Well then," he said, "I'll tell you how the land lies in there and where to go to find the game."

"That's good, *Uduji*," said Young Puppy. "*Wado.*"

Hiadeoni gathered small pieces of wood with his good left hand. Grey Owl had two good hands, but with his bad leg, it was difficult for him to wander around looking for wood. It was late in the day, and Hiadeoni thought that they should stop and camp before the night fell. He thought that they had gotten far enough away from the land of the Cave People to stop and rest in safety. He hoped so. He knew that Grey Owl's wound as well as his own needed attention, and both of them needed rest.

As he gathered small sticks in his one good hand, Hiadeoni tried to imagine his return trip to the land of the Cave People. He saw himself leading a large number of his own people against a town. He saw the town in flames, and he and his followers were killing the entire population.

But even as he indulged his imagination in this way, his mind told him that it was very likely that no one would follow him again, that after this disastrous defeat was known back home, he would be publicly chastised and privately shunned. Besides, his right arm might never work again. What kind of a war leader would he be?

He walked back to where Grey Owl waited beside the small stream, and he dropped the wood to the ground beside the tiny fire that Grey Owl had already kindled. They did their best to doctor each other's wounds, but they were severely limited in what they could do. Then, exhausted from travel, pain and the loss of blood, they lay down to rest. Soon both men were asleep.

Hiadeoni came quickly awake to the sound of loud noises unlike any he had ever heard before. At first he did not believe his own eyes. He thought that he must be having some sort of vision, induced, perhaps, by his pain and loss of blood. He had never seen anything like the frightening sight which startled him wide awake. Seven men mounted on the backs of beasts. Six of the men had white faces and hands and hair growing on their faces. Behind the seven mounted men were more beasts. They reminded him of moose, but they were fatter, and they lacked the heavy antlers.

Then he realized what it was looming there before his eyes. He had heard tales of the strange white men with hairy faces who rode on the backs of large beasts. They came across the great waters in large boats, and they slaughtered people indiscriminately. They were like monsters. Trembling, he shook Grey Owl by the shoulder.

"Grey Owl," he said, "wake up. Run."

He had lost his war club when his shoulder had been smashed, and he had no other weapon with which to defend himself against these strange creatures. He stood up and started to run. Looking back, he saw that Grey Owl had struggled to his feet, but trying to run on his bad leg, had fallen down again. The strangers were moving closer, headed right into the campsite of the two wounded men.

Well, nothing had gone well for Hiadeoni since the ambush in the land of the Cave People, so he decided that at least he would die bravely. He would run no more. He would not abandon Grey Owl to die there alone at the hands of these terrible strangers. He hurried back to the side of his companion and knelt. He helped Grey Owl up to a sitting position, and both men stared ahead at the strangers.

"What are they?" asked Grey Owl. "Do you know?"

"They must be some of the white men we've been hearing about," said Hiadeoni.

"Ah yes," said Grey Owl. "Help me to my feet. At least we'll die fighting."

Riding at the head of the small group, Jacques Tournier raised his right hand in a sign of peace.

"N'avez pas peur, mes amis," he said. "We mean you no harm."

The two men there in front of him seemed to be braced for an attack, and they certainly had not understood his language. He could see that both men were badly wounded. Tournier turned for help to Little Black Bear.

"S'il vous plaît," he said, "see if you can talk to them."

Little Black Bear tried first the trade language, common in that part of the country, but he got no response. He tried several other languages with no success. He looked at Tournier.

"They're not from anywhere around here," he said in French.

"Then where?" said Tournier. "Do you have any idea?"

Little Black Bear thought for a moment. He looked at the two men and studied them.

"Um," he said. *"Peut-être . . ."*

He swung a leg over the back of his horse and slid easily to the ground. Then he took a couple of steps toward the two men. They stiffened and he stopped.

"Are you," he said, speaking the language of *Ga-ne-ah-*

go-oh-noh, the People of the Flint, "are you of the Extended Lodge?"

Tournier could see the surprise come into the eyes of the two wounded men, and he wondered what Little Black Bear had said.

"Yes," said Hiadeoni. "We are People of the Great Hill."

"I'm Little Black Bear of the Catawbas," said the interpreter. "Relax. We mean you no harm. Don't be afraid of these white men. They're friends."

He turned to face Jacques Tournier.

"These men are Senikas," he said in French. "They're part of the Great League from north of here. *La Ligue d'Iroquois.*"

"Ah," said Tournier. "*Bon. Bon.* Tell them, *s'il vous plaît*, that we have a *docteur* with us, and we would be pleased to have him treat their injuries."

Little Black Bear translated Tournier's offer into the language of the Flint People, which was close enough to that of the People of the Great Hill for mutual understanding. Hiadeoni looked at Grey Owl.

"What do you think?" he asked.

"Just now," said Grey Owl, "we thought they were going to kill us. What do we have to lose?"

Hiadeoni hesitated a brief moment longer, then relented. Little Black Bear translated, and Tournier immediately dismounted, a broad smile on his face.

"Dismount," he said. "Everyone. We will make camp here with these new friends. Docteur DuBois, please see to their wounds. Georges, prepare the evening meal, and serve these Iroquois first. *Allons. Allons.*"

Fourteen

I HAD HOPED on this expedition," said Jacques Tournier, addressing his entire company, "to have the chance to visit in the great nation of the *Chalaques,* but it seems that the *Chalaques* are still determined to maintain their *isolationnisme.* But *destinée* has now delivered us into the hands of these two new friends, and we can help each other. *C'est bon.*

"While the *Chalaques* are a powerful people and *certainement* would make important allies for *le Roi de France,* the time, it seems, is not quite right for us to meet with them. *Eh bien.* We won't give up our plans. We make adjustments and take advantage of the opportunities that come our way. We will come back to the *Chalaques* at a later date, when the time is right, and they are ready to accept strangers into their land.

"In the meantime, *mes amis,* just as important as the mission we are now postponing, perhaps even more so, is the friendship of and possible alliance with the great and powerful *Ligue d'Iroquois*, and here we have been handed this golden opportunity. We will take good care of these two wounded men, our new Iroquois friends, and escort them safely back to their homes."

Little Black Bear made this new offer from Tournier clear to Hiadeoni and Grey Owl, and the two men had only a brief conference before responding. They were more than pleased to accept. They had not actually said so to each other, but neither one had really thought that they had much chance of ever reaching home alive. They were too badly hurt to defend themselves if attacked or even to hunt for food, and they had a long way to travel. Now with this mighty escort of mounted white men, they just might make it.

Tournier ordered the camp packed up and ready to move, and he had two horses brought forward for the wounded men to ride. With a little persuasion and encouragement from Little Black Bear, Hiadeoni allowed himself to be put onto the back of one horse, but when they tried to get Grey Owl mounted, they found that the pain in his wounded leg was too much for him to endure.

Then at the suggestion of Little Black Bear, they constructed a drag. It was modeled on the same type, he explained, that generations of his people had used, attached to dogs to carry things for them. All they had to do was make a larger one so that Grey Owl could be placed on it. Then he could be dragged along in relative comfort by one of the *chevaux*.

Two long poles were cut and tied together an arm's length from the smaller ends. They were then laid across the back of a horse with the longer ends of the poles trailing behind on the ground. Between the trailing poles, blankets and skins were stretched and secured, and on that cot, Grey Owl was laid out on his back and covered over to keep him warm. Tournier called this fabrication a travois, and he was very pleased with it. That problem solved, the company headed north.

Young Puppy was pleased. The land was just as his uncle had described it to him. He had traveled through the woods to the southwest of Turkey Town until he had arrived at a large clearing, created by the Real People to attract the deer and other grazing animals. Something would show up soon. It always did.

Young Puppy made his way slowly and quietly up to the edge of the field, for it was a new area to him, and he was not hunting deer, in spite of what he had told his uncle. He was looking for an enemy to kill, and if one should be out there, he didn't want the man to find him first.

The pasture was empty of game when Young Puppy arrived there, so he hid himself and watched and waited. It wasn't long before he saw some deer come into the field to graze, but he left them alone. Any other time he would have been sorely tempted. Then, when the sky began to darken, he returned to Turkey Town.

"You saw no deer?" asked his disappointed uncle.

"I saw some," said Young Puppy, choosing his words carefully so as not to tell a lie, "but I didn't get a shot."

He followed this same procedure for the next three days, always with the same results. Gusa-dihi was puzzled. He had expected better things from his nephew. Each day he offered to go with Young Puppy, and each day he was refused. The fifth day out, with the sun still low in the morning sky, Young Puppy was watching a small herd of deer grazing contentedly in the middle of the field.

He heard a dull thud, and the suddenness and unexpectedness of it startled him, and he saw the big male deer leap forward, only to collapse on its front legs, then roll over on one side and lie still. An arrow protruded from its shoulder.

He tensed and waited. He had not known that anyone else was near. Then from across the way, a man came running out into the open. He had a bow in one hand and a knife in the other. He ran to the side of the dead or dying animal, knelt and quickly slit its throat.

"A *Gusa?*" Young Puppy asked himself hopefully. He was certain that the man was not one of the Real People. He sucked in a deep breath, hefted his war club in his right hand and stepped boldly out into the open.

"What are you?" he called out, speaking in the language of the Real People.

The man stiffened, surprised. Then he stood and turned to face his challenger, his bloody knife still in his right hand, and a dark scowl on his face. Young Puppy judged him to be a man, not quite as old as Gusa-dihi, but certainly older than Asquani. His face and body were covered with tattoos. Young Puppy had certainly challenged a formidable foe.

Then the man said something which Young Puppy did not understand.

"This land belongs to the Real People," Young Puppy said. "You have no right to be here."

"You're a *Chalakee?*" the man said, suddenly shifting to the trade language. Young Puppy understood. His command of the trade language was fairly good.

"Yes," he said. "What are you?"

"I'm a *Cusa*," said the man, using the jargon word for his own people.

"Go back where you came from then," said Young Puppy, "and leave that deer behind. It belongs to the *Chalakees*, like everything else on this land. You're hunting on *Chalakee* land."

The *Gusa* dropped his bloody knife to the ground and took the war club away from the belt around his waist. He held it up before him, ready to fight.

"Come and see whose deer it is," he said.

Young Puppy raised his own club high above his head and gobbled like a turkey, and the *Gusa* man yelled and jumped over the body of the deer, running straight toward Young Puppy. Young Puppy ran to meet him. Halfway between the trees and the fresh kill, they met. The war clubs clashed together and crossed, each checking the other's forward motion. The *Gusa* spun on his right foot, moving around behind Young Puppy, and his left arm circled Young Puppy's throat.

Young Puppy pulled at the arm with his left hand, but it was tight around him. The clubs were still tangled overhead. Young Puppy gasped and choked. He moved a foot back between the *Gusa*'s legs and hooked it around one of the man's ankles. Then he kicked forward with all his might and threw all his weight backward at the same time. Both men went over. The *Gusa* landed hard on his back with the weight of Young Puppy crashing down against his chest. The sudden, hard impact caused him to loosen his hold around Young Puppy's neck and to drop his club. Young Puppy rolled quickly to his right and scrambled to his feet.

The *Gusa* turned over onto his hands and knees and was reaching for his war club when he saw Young Puppy running toward him. Leaving the club on the ground, he raised himself up onto his knees and braced himself for the rush. As Young Puppy came near, the *Gusa* reached out with both hands, gripped him around the waist and heaved, and Young Puppy felt himself flung up and over, the momentum of his own running body aiding the toss. He ducked his head and rolled as he landed, coming back up to his feet. As he turned to face his foe, the *Gusa* picked up his war club and stood ready again.

"Come on, little *Chalakee*," he said. "I tossed you like a feather, and I'll break you like a stick."

Young Puppy began to sidle to his left, and the *Gusa* countered. They circled, moving closer to each other with each round. Then the *Gusa* stepped in quickly and made a sudden sideways swipe with his club. Young Puppy ducked low, and he heard the sound of the club slicing air just above his head.

He made a short jab with his own club, driving it hard into the *Gusa*'s stomach, causing him to double over and expel his breath loudly. Young Puppy straightened up and raised his knee at the same time, striking the *Gusa* in the chest and knocking him over backward. He moved quickly, landing on the *Gusa*'s chest as soon as the man hit the ground, and he swung fast and hard. His first blow glanced off the side of the *Gusa*'s head, stunning him. The second crushed his skull.

Slowly Young Puppy stood up. Breathing hard, he looked down at his latest victim. He was triumphant, and he was alone. No older, more experienced man had led him to this victory. He had accomplished his purpose.

• • • •

Guwisti was anxious for the women of both clans to reach a decision. She had asked her mother over and over to give her an idea of how the talks were going, but Diguhsgi, the Weaver, would not tell her daughter anything.

"When it's been decided, I'll let you know," she said.

Guwisti found it all terribly frustrating. She even sometimes thought that her mother was tormenting her on purpose. Still she took every opportunity to tell her mother how she felt about Young Puppy, and to brag about his looks and his abilities.

"What other young man among the Real People has a *sogwili?*" she asked. "Only Asquani, and he's not so young. Besides, he already has a wife. And how many men as young as Young Puppy have gone clear to the land of the *Ani-Senika* and killed our enemies up there? Not many, I think. And besides all that, Mother, I love Young Puppy. If you don't get them all to agree to this match, I'll never marry anyone. Never."

"Be patient, Guwisti," Diguhsgi said. "We're still exchanging gifts between the Long Hair People and the Bird People. We'll come to an agreement soon enough. Besides all that, what's your rush? You're young. You have many years ahead of you."

With her cousins and aunts she had similar conversations. What was taking them so long, she asked. Had they not made up their minds? Were young women always tormented like this before they married? Or was it maybe the fault of the Long Hair women? Did they think that she was not good enough for Young Puppy? Could that be it?

"Not good enough for him?" said one. "Why, he's no different from the rest. A man's a man. That's all."

"He is different," said Guwisti. "He's more handsome, and he's brave. And he loves me and treats me well."

"Enjoy it while you can," said another. "All that will change after you're married."

All the women laughed, all except Guwist'.

"It won't be that way with us," she said. "But we might be old and feeble before you make up your minds."

"What's your hurry?" said an older aunt. "Is your *alesta* itching you that bad?"

"And you want Young Puppy to scratch that itch?"

Again they laughed, but still Guwisti saw no humor in the jokes. They irritated her, and that was all.

"I wish that you would come to a decision soon with the Long Hair women," she said, suddenly changing her tone. She was calm and dignified. "I just want to get started on my house. I'd like to get the work done before the cold sets in. That's all."

But she didn't fool the women of the Bird Clan, not a bit. They all knew that Guwisti was anxious to have her man.

Fifteen

HER NAME was Uyona, or Horn, like the horn of *yansa*, the buffalo. It was an unusual name for a woman, but then, Uyona was an unusual woman. She was old, so old that the people were afraid of her and suspicious. No one, they thought, should live to be that old. The Real People were great respecters of age, but only up to a point. There was such a thing as excess, even in the time one spent on earth. And excessive age was something to be wary of.

It was commonly known that there were some old ones, raven mockers, *Golanuh Ahyelisgi*, they were called, who had the power to extend their own lives well beyond the normal span by stealing what was left of the lives of others. That time could then be added to their own.

Because it was so much easier for them, they stole from those who were already weak: the sick or wounded, old ones almost ready to die, very young ones who had not yet developed any strength, anyone in a weakened condition.

It would be too much of a struggle to try to steal the life away from a strong, healthy person.

If a raven mocker stole the remaining life away from a dying old man, he would add only a very short time to his own life, but stealing from an infant, he might add years.

Raven, *Golanuh*, was a war title given to experienced warriors who had killed a number of enemies of the Real People. Taking the form of a raven, the raven mocker killed too, but in a sneaking and cowardly way, mocking the real *Golanuh*.

Naturally, a raven mocker would never admit to being such a despicable thing, but people still knew that such creatures existed. Therefore anyone among them who lived to a seemingly unnatural old age was in danger of becoming an object of fear and suspicion. Quietly, people said things to one another.

"How does old Horn keep on living? Do you know? She's so old."

"Do you suppose she stole away the life of your cousin's *usdi*? The one that was lost just four days ago?"

"Have you seen her lately? She's horrible-looking. I've never seen anything so ugly."

"It frightens me to look at her."

"Did she take the last bit of life from old Wrinkle Skin as he lay dying in his bed?"

The questions always went unanswered. The people stopped short of actually accusing Uyona of being a real raven mocker. But they were certainly afraid of her. They were suspicious of her too. And she knew. She knew what they thought about her. She had known for a long time. Because of that, she lived alone in a house outside the walls of Kituwah and far into the woods.

She felt safe out there alone. If the people saw her every day, if she lived in town among them, they would be reminded too often of their fears, and the occasional questions might change to direct accusations. Once that happened, they might decide to go ahead and kill her and burn her body in her house. She had seen it happen to others a few times in her long life.

But people did come to see her occasionally. They came, not to visit, and not because they enjoyed her company, but because they knew that she had certain knowledge and certain powers. They came to see her only when they needed her help or advice, and that was another reason they left her mostly alone, in spite of their evil suspicions. They knew that now and then, they would need her.

Almost everyone in Kituwah had been to see her at least once, and some of them had visited several times. There were also those who came from other towns, traveling great distances to seek her help. Always they were afraid, but when they came to see her, they were usually so desperate that they managed to overcome their fear for a time.

She enjoyed looking at them when they came. They would sit stiff and nervous and frightened, waiting for her to give them the mixture of herbs or the words of wisdom and power which they needed. When she finally served them (and, of course, she always did), they would thank her quickly and rush away, relieved to be getting out safely —and alive.

She had outlived six husbands, and she had fought in wars against the *Ani-Senika*, the *Ani-Gusa*, the *Ani-Sawahoni, Ani-Chahta, Ani-Chiksa* and other enemies of

Ani-yunwi-ya, the Real People. She had killed her enemies in battle.

And yes. She had even been there that time the Real People rose up in violent rebellion against their own *Ani-Kutani* and wiped them out to a man. And she had killed a priest or two herself. No one else was left alive who even remembered that time, and many did not even know the stories about it anymore. In her youth, she had been both beautiful and strong. But no one was alive who remembered that either.

She had borne twelve children, and she had outlived them all. She had even outlived some of her grandchildren. The ones remaining were all grown and had families of their own. Even they rarely came to see her. Even they were afraid of her. None of them would go inside her house, so great was their fear.

When she thought back over her many long years, which she did but rarely, it seemed to her that she had been many different women, that she had led many different lives. And how did she feel now that she was old and alone? Did she hate the people because of their fear and suspicion? Was she lonely? Was she bitter that they had forgotten the days of her youth? No. She was simply living the last of the series of lives that had been given her by the powers above. She did not especially love that life, nor did she hate it. It was her lot. She lived it. And when her time came round, she would die.

It was to Uyona then that Diguhsgi went when the women of the Long Hair Clan and those of the Bird Clan had at last agreed. The marriage between Young Puppy and Guwisti was all right with them, but there was one thing left to do before the final decision could be made. Some-one with the power to see into the future must be consulted, someone who could tell the women whether or not this match would prove to be satisfactory. Uyona was widely known to have such powers.

"My daughter is thinking of marriage," Diguhsgi said. She sat on a stump beneath an arbor just outside the old woman's house. The house, she couldn't help but notice, was badly in need of repair. Worn-out baskets, pieces of broken pots, bones and bits of hide from small animals and other kinds of trash lay all around.

"*Uh?*" said the old woman.

"My daughter's name is Guwisti. She's a Bird Person."

"*Uh.*"

"The young man is called Young Puppy. He's a Long Hair person from Stikoyi."

"*Uh,*" said Uyona. She knew both of the young people, and she also knew their clans, but she didn't bother saying this to Diguhsgi. She would let the woman tell her all as if she knew nothing. In fact, she had known about the discussions taking place between the women of the two clans. She had known all along, and she had been waiting for Diguhsgi to come to see her. She had known that she would.

"I came to seek your advice about this proposed match," said Diguhsgi. "Will it be a good one?"

"Come back to see me in four days," said the old woman. She said no more. The interview was at an end. Diguhsgi knew that, and she got up and walked away. She did not know what Uyona would do in the next four days to arrive at her judgment. She might go to the water and create a tiny whirlpool with her hand and watch while a leaf floated through it. She might possess an *ulunsuti*, a powerful transparent crystal from the forehead of an *uk'ten'*. If so, she might gaze into it and see something there. Or she might have some other method, something Diguhsgi knew nothing about. Whatever her method, she would give the right answer. Uyona had never been known to be wrong.

In spite of the fact that they were still traveling, and their wounds had not yet healed, both Hiadeoni and Grey Owl were feeling much better. Their wounds were improving, thanks to the attentions of the French *docteur*, and their spirits were higher than they had been before. They were confident that with the help of Jacques Tournier and his company, they would make it back home safely.

Of course, they still would have to face their people, the friends and families of the ones who had been killed, and they were not looking forward to that sad task. They knew that they might even be blamed for the deaths. No. It was certain that they would be blamed. Hiadeoni was especially vulnerable in that respect, for he had been the one who had encouraged the others to join him on this ill-fated raid.

Still they were feeling better than before. Hiadeoni thought that even if his reputation should suffer because of the loss of lives, it might be restored at least somewhat by his bringing home these white men as new friends and allies. They could be valuable friends, he thought. They had many things that would be helpful to his people. They had knives, both short and long, that were much harder and sharper than anything his people had. They had pots made of some kind of hard metal. They had tightly woven warm blankets of many different and very bright colors. They had the big animals which they called *chevaux*. One could load their backs with supplies, or one could ride on their backs. And they had fire sticks that made a loud noise and could kill at great distances. They had short ones shaped like horns and longer ones which took both hands to fire. And they were interested in trade. Hiadeoni was hopeful that his new association with these men would help to offset the shame of his failed raid on the Cave People.

They were about halfway home, according to Hiadeoni's estimate, when they started to ford a small river. Grey Owl's leg was doing well enough that he was able to get himself off the travois and onto the back of a horse, long enough for the crossing. The bank on the opposite side of the tree-lined river had a well-used trail cutting its way through. They were in the middle of the river when the attack came.

They appeared almost magically from behind trees and from bushes, and their terrifying shrieks were heard as soon as the painted warriors were seen. At the same time an arrow struck one of the Frenchmen in the chest, and he fell backward off his *cheval* into the water. Other arrows flew. Hiadeoni and Grey Owl recognized these people as their enemies. So did the Catawba interpreter.

"*Ofo*," shouted Little Black Bear.

Another Frenchman fell as the *Ofo* warriors ran into the water swinging their ball-headed war clubs.

"*Déchargez*," shouted Tournier, and he raised his *pistolet*, thumbed back the hammer and pulled the trigger. Sparks flew and black powder ignited with a loud poof, sending out a cloud of smoke. An *Ofo* warrior running directly toward Tournier stopped in his tracks and looked down at a small hole in his chest. Looking up at Tournier with a terrible question painted on his face, he swayed back, then forward, then fell facedown into the water.

Other guns sounded, and other *Ofo* attackers fell. Those not killed outright, both unhurt and wounded, turned and ran. They had been totally surprised by the French weapons. Hiadeoni and Grey Owl were amazed.

"I am glad that these men are our friends," Hiadeoni said to Grey Owl, and both men were more convinced than ever that their people should form an alliance with the French.

Tournier's company picked up their dead and finished crossing the river. They rode on through the woods to a clearing, and then they stopped. Two Frenchmen had been killed. Two were wounded. While the *docteur* tended to the hurt, others buried the dead. Hiadeoni and Grey Owl, speaking through Little Black Bear, gave Tournier their heartiest congratulations.

"I regret," said Tournier, "that they attacked us without warning. I would much rather have had the opportunity to speak with them and assure them that our intentions are peaceful. Sadly, they gave us no choice."

"The *Ofo* are no good," said Little Black Bear. "It's just as well that things happened as they did. We should have pursued them and killed them all."

But Tournier was not convinced.

"We lost lives too," he said. The purpose of his expedition was to establish trade relations. In order to do that, he had to make friends first. Then he had to make allies of his new friends. The senseless fighting and killing saddened him.

Sixteen

ACCOMPANIED by his uncle, Gusa-dihi, Young Puppy arrived back in Stikoyi the day after his mother had visited Uyona. After warmly greeting her brother, Lolo told her anxious son about the progress.

"The women of both clans have all agreed," she said, "and in three more days, I'll go back to see old Horn for her advice. If she says that the match will be good, then it will happen."

Young Puppy was elated. He knew that the match was perfect, and Guwisti knew it too. How could the old woman say otherwise? Only three more days and they would be able to begin the preparations. It would still take some time before he and Guwisti could actually become man and wife. The women of the Bird Clan in Kituwah would have to help Guwisti build her new house. Young Puppy would have to hunt and bring back a deer. There were other details. Still he was happy, for in just three days they would begin. He knew they would.

He was also happy that his uncle had come back with him to Stikoyi, for it made his mother happy to see her brother again. Young Puppy was also pleased with his own renewed acquaintance with his uncle. But most of all, he was happy because Gusa-dihi would verify his tale of the killing of the *Gusa* who was trespassing in the hunting grounds of the Real People. Now everyone would know that Young Puppy, alone, unassisted and uninstructed, had killed an enemy, and perhaps he would get a new name.

The old woman sat before a small fire in front of her house. She was alone, and she knew that she would not be bothered, for it was well after dark. No one was brave enough to venture near her house after dark. And it was important that she not be disturbed, for she was engaged in very important business.

She had built her fire of seven specific different kinds of wood, and she had kept it going for some time, long enough to have both ashes and glowing embers. To her right and to her left sat small pots and baskets containing parts of various plants: stems, roots, leaves, all dried. Poked in between her tight and wrinkled old lips was a short pipe, the stem a piece of river cane, the small bowl made of clay. Just behind the bowl sat the small molded figure of a tree frog, facing the smoker.

There was a chill in the night air, but it did not bother Uyona. She sat close to her small fire, and its warmth, combined with her general toughness, was enough. She sucked at her pipe stem, sending up a few last clouds of smoke toward the heavens. The small amount of ancient, sacred tobacco in the bowl was consumed.

She took the pipe in her hand, holding it by the hot

bowl, and turned it over above the fire, allowing the loose dottle to drop into the flames. Then she put the pipe down on the ground beside her. She reached into a clay pot and took out a pinch of the dried contents, sprinkling them into the fire. The fire hissed and shot out sparks, and she muttered a few words. A person sitting across the fire from her would not have been able to hear her clearly enough to understand.

She reached into a basket and brought something out which she rubbed between her palms, crushing it into tiny pieces. She tossed that into the fire and watched closely. The material was consumed by the flames, but nothing spectacular happened. The wrinkles in her forehead deepened as she knit her brow.

She poked a bony finger just short of the flames, and she moved some glowing embers around. She frowned a bit more deeply. She did not yet like what she saw.

From another basket she withdrew a strangely shaped root. It was dark, dry, gnarled and twisted. Carefully she placed it in the fire, and she watched it as it blackened. Writhing like something alive and in pain, it transformed itself into a variety of shapes before the flames reduced it to ashes.

Then Uyona, the Horn, heaved a deep sigh of resignation. She picked up her pipe once again and refilled the bowl from a pouch which lay there by her side. With the forefinger and thumb of her left hand, she picked up a small glowing ember and dropped it into the bowl for a light. Soon she was puffing away contentedly, sending clouds of aromatic smoke up toward the spirits who lived on the other side of the Sky Vault.

She sat there until the fire had died out completely, and

then she smoothed the bed of ashes with her hands. At last, she moved all of the pots and baskets, along with her pipe and tobacco pouch, back into the house. It was late, and she needed some sleep. The woman would be coming to see her again tomorrow, and she wanted to be ready for her when she came.

Young Puppy sat inside the townhouse with a group of men. They lounged around a central fire smoking and telling tales, and for the first time, Young Puppy heard about the most recent party of *Ani-Senika* who had tried to invade the country of the Real People over near Kituwah. The Wolves had ambushed them and defeated them soundly.

"It seems that there were six of them," the tale teller said, "and our Wolves killed four. The other two were badly hurt, but they escaped."

"The Wolves let them go on purpose," said another.

"Yes," admitted the teller, "because they thought that those two would never make it back to their homes anyway, and even if they did, they would have to tell their own people how badly they were beaten by the Real People."

So the Senikas dared to try again, thought Young Puppy. Even after what 'Squani and I did to them in their own land. If they had any sense, he told himself, they would stay home. We killed them there, and we killed them here. How many lessons, he wondered, did they need? He thought that perhaps someone should go up there just one more time to make it very clear to them that the Real People were not to be taken lightly.

The story of the Senikas having been told, someone brought up the latest exploit of Young Puppy, and once again he was obliged to relate his own adventures on the frontier between Turkey Town and the country of the *Ani-Gusa*. He did not mind the retelling.

Diguhsgi saw the old woman waiting for her as she approached the house. For her daughter's sake, she was anxious to hear the news, but the sour expression on Uyona's face made her worry. Old Horn always looks like that though, she thought, trying to reassure herself.

"Sit down," said Uyona.

Diguhsgi sat on a stump of a tree out in the open in front of the house. She was facing the old woman, who sat on a bench leaning back against the front wall of her house. A smooth circle of ashes lay on the ground between the two women. Diguhsgi waited, but Uyona said nothing. Instead, calmly and slowly, she filled and lit her pipe. Clouds of smoke momentarily obscured her face from her visitor's vision.

"Uyona," said Diguhsgi, her voice hesitant and timid, "can you tell me now? Will the match be good between Young Puppy and Guwisti?"

"It will be good," said the old woman, "but not now."

"What? I don't understand."

"Build your daughter's house, and tell her to make it her home. Tell her to move into her new house as soon as it is built, but tell her also that she will live in it alone for one year. For Young Puppy will have a year of trial. He will be like a dead man, and then he will be reborn. Only then will the match be good. *Gayule jiwonuh.*"

She had said all that she would say. With a heavy heart, Diguhsgi stood up to leave.

"*Wado*, Uyona," she said. She placed on the stump the

tobacco that would pay for the service she had received. Then she turned to walk away.

"Mother," said Guwisti, "what did she say?"

Diguhsgi's heart was heavy, for she was bringing bad news to her daughter. She tried to look at Guwisti without a long face, but Guwisti could see that something was wrong. Immediately she thought the worst.

"She said no?" she asked. "What's wrong? Did she say why?"

"Daughter," said Diguhsgi, "let's go somewhere where we can be alone. I'll tell you everything."

They walked to the river's edge, and Diguhsgi made Guwisti sit down. There she told her everything the old woman had said to her.

"One year?" said Guwisti.

"One year alone in your house," said her mother.

"But why?"

"I told you. She said that Young Puppy will be facing a trial, and he will have to be reborn."

"What does that mean?" said Guwisti. "To be reborn? How can he be reborn? Will he die and then be born again —a baby? And then must I wait for him to grow old enough for me?"

"I don't know," said Diguhsgi. "I don't think that's what she meant."

"And what kind of trial must he endure? For what reason?"

"That was all she said. I know this news upsets you, but try to think about the good part. She said the match will be good. Young Puppy will be your husband."

"In a year from now," said Guwisti. "Why does the old

woman have to talk in riddles anyway? And why do we have to listen to her advice? She may be just a crazy old woman. Or worse."

Diguhsgi stood up to face her daughter.

"Be careful how you talk about Uyona," she said. "Besides, whatever you or I may think of her, the other women, of both clans, will never agree to go against her advice. I wish it could be the way you want it to be, but you and Young Puppy will have to wait."

When the news reached Young Puppy over in Stikoyi, he went to the river and sat there alone. He did not want to see anyone. He was angry and frustrated. He could see no reason to wait. He wanted Guwisti and she wanted him. The women of both clans had agreed. Now this old woman was spoiling everything, and he wished that she was dead. Why had Guwisti's mother gone to that old woman anyway?

He thought about going to Kituwah to see Guwisti and talk with her. They could run away together, and she could build her house in the Bird Clan area of another town, a town far away, Turkey Town perhaps. They could go back home with Gusa-dihi when he left. No one could stop them.

But then, of course, no one would approve of such actions either, and they would be estranged from both their families. Gusa-dihi probably wouldn't even let them travel with him. Young Puppy wondered if he and Guwisti could be happy living that way, and he wondered if she would even agree to such a thing.

And then, of course, he wondered too, in spite of himself, if the old woman really could see into the future, and if the events of the next year really did hold some terrible ordeal in store for him. If so, what could it be? A life like death, following which he must be reborn. It made no sense. It couldn't be. The old woman was either crazy or vindictive. He wondered which it was.

And then he thought that maybe he just hadn't done enough to make himself a man. After all, no one, not even his mother's brother, had suggested that he be given a new name, a man's name, a warrior's name in recognition of his deeds.

Well, he thought, he would have to do something to pass the time. He couldn't simply sit around and wait for the year to pass. He would only think about Guwisti all the time, and it would make him crazy, as crazy as old Uyona. So what would he do?

He decided that he would busy himself with doing great deeds and earning a worthy name. When the time had passed and his wedding day came, he would not be married as Young Puppy, but as—someone else. He would have a warrior's name.

He thought about going back to Turkey Town with his uncle, and then he thought about the Senikas again. He thought about their latest raid. He recalled his own earlier thought that they needed to be taught a final lesson. Well, he would give it to them. He alone. He would ride his *sogwili* north into the heart of the land of the *Ani-Senika*, and he would deal them a powerful blow, striking one place and riding fast to another to strike again. He would pay them a visit they would never forget, and the Real People would talk and sing about it for generations to come.

Yes. The *Ani-Senika*. And alone. It was far more daring than returning to Turkey Town with his uncle. It was much farther away, far to the north. He would be surrounded by enemies. Enemies who were fresh on people's minds. This bold plan would surely earn for him a new name.

Seventeen

THIS TIME he did not tell his mother where he was going. He did not tell anyone. He knew that his uncle would probably be gone by the time he returned, and he would not have seen him off. It was too bad, but it could not be helped. He packed what he would need for the long trip, and he tied it in a bundle which he strapped to the back of his *sogwili* just behind the saddle. He left early in the morning under cover of darkness, before anyone was up and going to the river to start their day. He knew, however, that he would have to say something to the Wolves. He would not be able to get past them unseen. It would be dangerous to try.

He decided that he would stop at Kituwah to see Guwisti. He would likely be gone for a long time and, although he felt confident in his own abilities, he had to admit that there was always the possibility he would not come back. He thought about Uyona's strange prophecy

again, that he would die and be reborn. Ah well, anything
could happen, he guessed. But still, he had to see Guwisti.
Besides, he had not talked with her, had not seen her, since
the bad news from old Horn. He wondered how she had
taken it.

And there was another advantage in stopping at Kituwah
for a visit. By the time he reached Kituwah and took the
time to talk with Guwisti, then finally got started on his
trip, it would be daylight. There would be less chance of
the Wolves mistaking him for someone trying to slip
through their lines. He was looking for a fight, but not
with them.

By the time he reached Kituwah, the sun was beginning
to light up the eastern sky. He left his *sogwili* outside the
wall and went into the town to look for his love. He wondered as he walked, after this visit how long would it be
before he would see her again? He wondered if he would
ever see her again.

Asquani sat on a flat rock on the side of the mountain
overlooking the road below. There were other Wolves
around, some not far from him, some clear across the pass.
He was looking forward to the middle of the day, for it
would be time for others to come and take over the watch.
It would be time for him to go home to Osa.

He thought about her often as he sat on the mountainside. He thought about the way she looked and the way
she felt to his touch, the smell of her hair and the sound of
her voice. And lately, of course, he thought about the
shape of her belly and the new life that was growing inside.
He wondered if it would be a girl or a boy, but he told

himself that it did not matter. He would be just as happy either way.

"Asquani."

He looked over his shoulder to see who had called his name, and there he saw Trotting Wolf walking toward him. He stood up and turned to greet the head warrior of the Wolf Clan.

"Yes," he said. "Do you want something of me?"

"You are the only one of us who has a *sogwili*," said Trotting Wolf.

"Yes. I know."

"I want you to ride to Stikoyi."

"*Howa*," said 'Squani.

"We have used all the Wolves from Kituwah too much here already. They've done more than their share. Now it's time for another change, and this time, I'd like to have some men come over from Stikoyi."

"I'll ride over and tell them," said 'Squani. "I think they'll come."

"Yes," said Trotting Wolf. "I think so too. If you want to go now, I will stay with the others and watch without you. When you're through at Stikoyi, you can just go on home to your wife. There won't be any need for you to come back up here."

"Well," said 'Squani, "I'll just go on then."

For a time he rode along the mountain path. There was a place on the other side of Kituwah where it was easier for the horse to go down. Passing it by, he looked down on his town, and he saw there outside the walls the horse of his friend Young Puppy. Ah, he thought, he is visiting his love. He thought that if Young Puppy was still there when he returned, he would visit with him awhile. He rode on to the place where the descent was easier, and there he rode down and into the road.

In a short time he reached Stikoyi, and he found the Wolves and talked to them. Enough agreed to go to the pass and relieve the Kituwah Wolves who had been watching there. 'Squani visited with them long enough to be polite, and they fed him. Then he started back along the road toward Kituwah, headed for home. He was anxious to lie down beside his wife and hold her in his arms. He wanted to place his hands on her belly to see if the *usdi* would kick.

Guwisti walked with Young Puppy outside the wall of the town to the place where he had left his horse. At first they said nothing, and they did not look at each other. They looked at the ground. They stroked the horse. Guwisti noticed the pack on the animal's back.

"Are you going somewhere?" she asked him.

"Yes."

"A long trip?"

"Yes."

"I'll miss you," she said. "I wish you didn't have to go."

"I couldn't stand to just sit around here and wait for the women to tell us when it's time. More than a year. I guess the old woman doesn't think I'm ready. I don't know. And I don't like it."

Guwisti shrugged.

"I don't like it either," she said. "She saw something bad in our future, I guess. But only for the next year. After that it will be all right."

"It will be all right unless I'm a baby and you're a grown woman," he said.

They both laughed, but Young Puppy's frown came back in a short time.

"What could it be?" said Young Puppy, and there was evidence of anger in his voice. "This thing in my future?"

"I don't know," said Guwisti.

"Well," he said, "whatever it is, I can't just hang around here and wait for it to happen. I have to do something. I have to keep myself busy." He paused for a moment. "I have to go away for a while."

"What will you do?" she asked him. "Where will you go?"

He didn't want his plans known. If he told Guwisti, she might tell her mother, and the word might get back around to his mother. He didn't want anyone to know what he was planning to do. He didn't want them to be worrying about him.

"I don't know," he said. "I'm just going out there. Maybe I'll hunt. Maybe I'll find the white men again, the ones who gave the *sogwilis* to Asquani and me. Maybe I'll trade with them. I don't know."

"Be careful," she said. "I don't want anything to happen to you, because—I'm going to be waiting for you."

"For a whole year?" he asked.

"Yes," she said. "For a whole year, if I must."

He climbed up into the saddle and rode off without another word. He rode toward the pass where the Wolves would be watching.

When Asquani reached Kituwah he was surprised to see that Young Puppy's horse was no longer there, for he had not passed the young man on the road. He had figured that Young Puppy had been visiting Guwisti and therefore would be returning to Stikoyi when he left. But if Young Puppy had gone back to Stikoyi, 'Squani would have passed him on the road.

Where could he have gone, he asked himself. The other direction along this road leads out of our country. Ah well, he's young, but he's a man, old enough to make his own decisions and to take care of himself. He could have gone anywhere. He might have taken the *sogwili* off the road and into a pasture somewhere for a fast ride. Young men do crazy things. There's no explaining their actions. He recalled the time when, in his own youth, he had left his parents in the night and gone to look for the *Ani-Asquani*. That had been a crazy thing to do. But he was glad that he had done it, for it was with the Spaniards that he had found his wife.

He put Young Puppy's erratic behavior out of his mind and went on home to see his wife. Outside the wall, he dismounted. He unsaddled the horse and left it to graze with the reins trailing on the ground. He was anxious to be with Osa, but he had to stop along the way to visit, however briefly, with those he met. On the way at last to his wife's house, he saw Guwisti.

" *'Siyo*, Guwist'," he said.

" *'Siyo*, 'Squan'."

"*Tohiju?*"

"Oh, I'm all right," she said. "I guess."

'Squani had been ready to hurry on by, but the sadness in her voice made him stop. It wasn't like her to be that way.

"Guwist'," he said, "is something wrong?"

"I don't know," she said. "Nothing really, I guess. I'm just worried."

He thought about Young Puppy's horse, and where the young man might have gone.

"Was Young Puppy here?" he asked.

"Yes."

"Did you talk with him?"

"Yes. We talked."

"Is that why you're worried? Something about Young Puppy?"

"He had a big bundle on the back of his *sogwili*," she said. "He's going on a trip. A long one. But he wouldn't tell me where he's going. Maybe hunting, he said. Or maybe to trade with the white men who gave you the *sogwilis*."

"Which way did he go?" asked 'Squani.

"Down the road," she said, pointing toward the way out of the land of the Real People, "that way."

'Squani thought that it was probably dangerous and therefore a little foolish on Young Puppy's part to go out that way to hunt. And it seemed utterly foolish for him to go out alone to look for the Frenchmen. None of it made sense. He tried not to show his concern to Guwisti.

"Well," he said, "don't worry too much. Young Puppy can take care of himself. I know. I've fought with him and hunted with him. And I don't think he'll stay away for very long. He'll be wanting to get back to you, I think. He's told me how he feels about you."

"He said he'll be gone a long time. He's angry, I think."

"At you?"

"No. But you know the women of our clans said that we could marry."

"Yes," said 'Squani. "I heard about that. It made me happy for you—and for Young Puppy."

"But my mother went to see Uyona, and the old woman said that we must wait for more than a year."

"Oh. Did she say why?"

"She said that Young Puppy will have a bad year," said Guwisti, "and that he will have to die and be reborn. Then, she said, everything will be all right for us."

A worried look came over the face of Asquani. He remembered his own hot-blooded youth, and he wondered what he might have done had someone told him that he had to wait a year to marry Osa.

"I think I understand why he's angry," he said. "I wonder what Uyona meant by what she said?"

"Young Puppy said that she must think that he's not ready yet. He said he couldn't just sit around and wait."

"And he didn't tell you where he was going or what he was planning to do?"

"No," she said. "Just what I told you. Nothing more than that."

Now 'Squani was worried. He had been forced to check the younger man's impulsiveness more than once when they had gone together to the Senika country. True, Young Puppy had done well enough in the end. He had learned much on that trip. He had even learned to be more patient, but then, 'Squani had been along to watch him and remind him. Alone, he might do anything that came into his mind.

He wondered where Young Puppy had gone and what

he was planning to do. Young Puppy's welfare had come to be of some importance to Asquani. He had grown to know and like the young man. He wanted to see Guwisti have a happy life with Young Puppy, plus he had entrusted the future of the writing to that impulsive young mind.

Eighteen

A T HIS WIFE'S HOUSE, 'Squani told Osa about Guwisti's worries, and about his own. She consoled him as best she could. She knew that he liked the young man, and, although she wasn't aware of the extent of her husband's concern, she knew somehow that he felt some sense of responsibility for Young Puppy.

"Try not to worry," she said.

"That's what I told Guwisti," he said.

They changed the subject and talked of their coming child. What if it was a boy? Since Osa had no brothers in Kituwah, who would teach him to be a man in the ways of the Real People and provide the discipline he would need while growing up?

"I'll do it myself," said 'Squani. "It's not the normal way, I know, but our situation here is not a normal one. I'll do it just the same."

When the sun was down and the night was dark, they crawled together under their big bear rug to go to sleep.

But 'Squani did not sleep right away. He was thinking about Young Puppy. Where could he have gone? And what could his plans be? He tried to imagine the young man's state of mind, his anger and frustrations, and he tried to put himself in Young Puppy's place. What would I have done, he asked himself, when I was that young and if those same things had happened to me?

He liked Young Puppy, of course, and was worried for his safety. But he also had another worry. For Young Puppy was the one he had chosen to pass along the writing to. At last, 'Squani fell asleep.

It was late into the night, and all was quiet. In the distance whippoorwills called, and the eerie hu hus of the owls sounded from the trees. Suddenly 'Squani sat up straight.

"Ha," he said out loud.

Osa stirred and came awake.

"What is it?" she asked. "Is something wrong?"

"No," he said. "Nothing is wrong. I think I know where he has gone."

Osa rubbed her sleepy eyes.

"Who are you talking about?" she asked.

"Young Puppy," he said. "I think I know where he is going and what he's planning to do. And I have to do something to try to stop him."

By the time Jacques Tournier's party reached the home of the two Senika warriors, the wounds of Hiadeoni and Grey Owl had almost healed. Hiadeoni's shoulder and arm were stiff, and Grey Owl walked with a decided limp, but he could walk, and he could ride unassisted on the back of one of the Frenchmen's *chevaux*. Both men had, in fact, become fairly accomplished riders.

There was much mourning for the men who had been lost, but the guests were seen to. They were fed and put up in a longhouse. Hiadeoni explained to them that following a few days of mourning, they would be able to talk to the town officials.

During the mourning time, Tournier had to keep close watch on his men, some of whom desperately wanted to pursue any of the young women in the town. He told them that any man caught with a Senika woman, or causing any kind of trouble in town, would be shot. He said that he would do it personally. The men grumbled, but they obeyed the orders.

Tournier was greatly relieved, though, when the period of mourning finally came to an end. Then a meeting of the town council was called, and Hiadeoni was made to relate the events of his raid and the cause of the deaths of his companions. There were women who had lost their husbands and children who had lost their fathers. This was not a matter to be taken lightly.

Tournier was able to watch the proceedings, and Little Black Bear was able to tell him most of what was being said. Tournier found their serious concern over the loss of a single life fascinating.

"At home," he said to Docteur DuBois, "if a soldier loses his life in battle, it is not seen as a matter of much importance. It seems to me that we could learn much from these simple people."

Then he noticed that the council not only failed to make any kind of decision regarding the matter, they did not even discuss it. Hiadeoni finished his tale, and the meeting broke up. That was all. Tournier asked Little Black Bear to explain this peculiarity.

"They have to go talk to their women," said the interpreter, "before they can make a decision."

"*Extraordinaire*," said Tournier, and he began to see that the *Indiens*, as he called them, were perhaps not such simple people as he had imagined them to be.

In another few days the council was reconvened, and the speaker made a long speech directed at Hiadeoni. In a shortened version, Little Black Bear told Tournier that Hiadeoni had been severely chastised. The lives and safety of the men who had followed him had been his responsibility, and he had failed them. Because of him, women were without husbands. Children cried for their fathers. Hiadeoni stood listening to this with his head hanging down in shame. At last the speaker told Hiadeoni what he must do to atone. He would hunt for the families which had lost their men, and he would have to pay them in other ways with a variety of goods. Hiadeoni agreed, and the matter was closed.

"But how will he be able to hunt," asked Tournier, "when his right arm is practically useless?"

Little Black Bear shrugged.

"He'll just have to find a way," he said.

"*Eh, excuse moi, mon ami*," said Tournier, "*mais*—does our Senika friend have to actually hunt? Or is he simply charged with providing a living for those unfortunate families whose men were lost?"

Little Black Bear thought for a moment before responding to that question.

"I think," he said, "that if he can find a way to provide for them without hunting, then it will be all right."

Tournier smiled and leaned back to relax.

"In that case," he said, "I'm sure that something can be worked out which will be satisfactory to all concerned."

Then the council turned to the matter of the visiting white men, a subject which Tournier was more than ready to listen to. He hoped, too, that he would be allowed to speak. Hiadeoni had already told of his meeting with them, how they had tended his and Grey Owl's wounds and brought them home, a long distance through sometimes hostile territory.

He told them that without the aid of these Frenchmen, he and Grey Owl would likely have died along with the others, and no one would have been left alive to tell the tale of what had happened on the ill-fated raid. He was deeply troubled and remorseful about the loss of his companions, and he accepted full responsibility, but at the same time he was grateful for the chance to face the council, even to his own shame, to at least be able to let people know what had happened to their loved ones. This opportunity, he said, he owed, they all owed, to Jacques Tournier.

Following some general discussion, the speaker pledged the friendship of the people of the town to the Frenchmen, and offered Tournier the chance to speak. Tournier gladly accepted the offer, and with Little Black Bear beside him, stood up before the crowd.

He told them he had come across the great waters from a faraway country called France. He told them that France was ruled over by a great King, and that he and all Frenchmen owed their loyalty to that King. He said that the King had charged him with the responsibility of meeting *Indiens* to make friends and form alliances for trade, and then he showed them some of the items that he would be able to offer them, should they agree.

As before, the council broke up without having made a decision. This time, Tournier was not surprised. He turned to Little Black Bear.

"They are going to talk to the women?" he said.

"*Oui, monsieur,*" the interpreter said.

Waiting for the council's decision, and assuming that it would be a favorable one, Tournier wondered what he should do about the *Chalaques* to the south. He felt good about his chances with the Iroquois, but he knew from the tale of Hiadeoni and Grey Owl that the two peoples were bitter enemies. He still wanted an alliance with the *Chalaques*, but he was not willing to give up his progress with their enemies to get it. It was a difficult situation. He would have to find a way to deal with it, for the Iroquois were the most powerful people in the north, and the *Chalaques* the most powerful in the south. His country would need the friendship of both if it would triumph in this new world over Spain.

During the next few days, while waiting for the council to reconvene, many of the people came around the Frenchmen to look at their weapons, their *chevaux*, and the other wonderful things they had. They felt the French cloth and studied their iron cooking pots. Tournier made sure that his men knew to allow the people to look at everything as closely as they wished.

"Let them see everything," he said. "Especially the women. Let them handle the cloth and the pots, anything that interests them. The more they see it and feel it and touch it, the more they will want it for themselves."

At last they were called back to the council. Tournier noticed that the spirits of Hiadeoni had much improved. And so were those of Jacques Tournier when he heard the decision. He had succeeded in making his first major alliance for his King. He called for a pack of goods to be brought into the longhouse and broken open, and he distributed pots and knives and cloth as gifts.

"When we come back to trade," he announced, "there will be much more."

The next day, Hiadeoni came to see Tournier. He looked at the Frenchman, then at Little Black Bear.

"Some of the warriors are talking about going back to the land of the Cave People," he said. "They don't like what happened down there. But others don't think that we should go back so soon. They sent me here to invite you to join the talk."

Tournier agreed, and he accompanied Hiadeoni back to the longhouse where the council meetings had taken place. This meeting did not seem to be a full council, but he noticed that some of the men present were the very ones he had noticed before as prominent, most notable among them the speaker of the council. They motioned for Tournier to sit down, and he did, Little Black Bear beside him.

"We suffered a bad defeat at the hands of the Cave People," the speaker said. "Some here want to go back there and balance things out. Some say that we should wait."

"It would be foolish to go now," said one.

"No," said another, "but it would be cowardly not to go. That's why we should. And we should go now."

The discussion continued for some time, and Tournier was again impressed by the behavior of these people. He noticed that no one ever interrupted another while he was speaking. No matter how strong the disagreement, everyone waited until a speaker was through before responding.

At last there was a lull in the talk, and the speaker turned to face Little Black Bear.

"What does our new friend think?" he asked.

Little Black Bear translated the question to Tournier. Tournier thought for a moment. Then he began to speak, slowly and carefully, pausing now and then to allow Little Black Bear to translate.

"If you do go back to the land of the *Chalaques*," he said, "whether now or at some later time, more of your people are likely to be killed. Even if you have success the next time, the *Chalaques* will surely come back here to retaliate once more. It seems to me that this terrible cycle of killing could go on and on forever. There will only be more women without husbands, more children without fathers.

"I think you should go back, but not to kill. I think you should go back and offer peace and put an end to all this killing between your peoples. What is its purpose anyway?"

Silence followed Tournier's oration. All eyes were on the floor. At last a man spoke up.

"If we are going to offer peace," he said, "we should only offer it after we have killed some of them, not after they have killed some of us."

"They wouldn't listen to any such proposal just after we had killed them," said another.

"Why should we want peace with the Cave People? We've been at war with them for as long as I can remember. Longer even. My grandfather fought the Cave People."

"Even if we should all agree that peace would be a good thing," said the speaker, "it would seem cowardly of us to propose it. And besides, if we sent a party to their land to talk of peace, the Cave People would most likely attack them before they had a chance to talk."

Tournier made a motion to indicate that he would like to speak again, and the speaker acknowledged him. Everyone else sat silent.

"Suppose," Tournier said, "that I go to them as envoy for you. I could tell them that you are willing to talk of peace. Then if they are willing, I can bring the word back to you. Only when both parties have agreed to meet and talk will you actually see each other face-to-face."

Following some murmurs and nodding of heads, the meeting broke up, as Tournier knew it would, with no decision having been made. But the next day Hiadeoni came to see the Frenchman.

"I bring word from our speaker," he said. "We want you to go to the Cave People to talk of peace."

Nineteen

OSA WAS ALONE AGAIN. Already she missed
Asquani. She had wanted to argue with him about
this trip, but she knew that it would do no good. The
safety of Young Puppy meant too much to him. He had
decided that the impulsive young man, angry and frustrated at the advice of Uyona and the decision of the clan
women to follow that advice, had ridden north to make a
lone raid on the *Ani-Senika.*

"He shouldn't try it by himself," he had said. "I'm going
to try to catch him before he's gone too far."

"Then you'll go on with him and fight some more?"
Osa had asked.

"No," 'Squani had said. "I'll try to talk him into coming
back with me. He's not properly prepared to fight and he's
gone for the wrong reasons. Besides that, there's no need
to attack the *Ani-Senika* just now. They came here last.
That's true. But we beat them soundly."

He had packed hastily for a long trip, taken his *sogwili*

and headed north. She hoped that he would do as he had said. She hoped that he would catch Young Puppy soon and bring him back. She hoped they wouldn't find a fight. She wanted 'Squani home with her. She wanted him safe—for herself—and for their coming *usdi*.

Diguhsgi and other women of the Bird Clan in Kituwah selected a site for Guwisti's new house. It was just down the row and not far from the house of Diguhsgi. They measured it out and marked the corners, and then they smoothed the ground. Soon they would cut trees and prepare poles with which to begin the actual construction.

Guwisti thought that she should have been excited at this time in her life, but the strange turn of events which began with the surprising and somewhat frightening pronouncement of old Uyona had dampened her spirits considerably. She smiled politely and thanked people for helping her, but she was just going through the motions, just doing what was expected of her. Nothing more.

She was getting her new house, her own house, so that she would have a place to bring her new husband. But she was to live in this new home alone for over a year, while he . . . Who knew what he would be doing all that time, or where he would be? Uyona's prediction had been vague but ominous.

And Young Puppy was not taking it well. He had been angry and pouting when last she had seen him, and he had gone off somewhere alone. He wouldn't say just where he was going or what he intended to do. Following the frightening words of the old woman, Guwisti would have preferred for Young Puppy to sit quietly and safely at home, or at least somewhere nearby, someplace where she could keep an eye on him and know that he was safe.

Asquani had told her not to worry, but she thought that she had detected at least a little concern in the expression on his face. And she was worried. She tried to keep herself busy with the women of her clan, but it did not help much. It did not keep her mind from imagining the dangers in Young Puppy's path and the long wait the two of them would have to endure. And then there was her own very uncertain future—with a man only just reborn.

And Young Puppy was faring no better. As he rode north toward the land of the *Ani-Senika*, his thoughts were on Guwisti. He longed for her. He ached. He hated the old woman for making such a foolish prediction. Why must he wait?

He would try to focus his anger on the *Ani-Senika*. This time, he told himself, he would stay longer in their country. He would kill more of them. Mounted on his *sogwili*, he would strike terror into their hearts. He could see them scattering before him as he rode hard, the turkey cry coming from deep in his lungs, his war club held high.

"I'll show them all," he said, and then he realized that his anger was not really directed at the Senika People. It was still aimed at his own people back home. He was just using the Senikas, as he would use an ax to cut a tree, as he used the *sogwili* to ride upon, as he used a robe to cover himself from the cold. So be it.

Jacques Tournier left the land of the Senikas feeling triumphantly cheerful. He had just made new, powerful, northern allies for his King, and he had high hopes of securing a similar alliance with the equally powerful *Chalaques* in the south. The Senika bid for peace, he thought, would provide him with the leverage he needed to get into the nation of the *Chalaques*, in spite of their determined isolationism, and talk with their leaders. He was not unknown to the *Chalaques*. He had a few friends among them. This should be relatively easy, he thought.

He had packed up his entire company and headed south with no Senika along for the trip. If the *Chalaques* saw him coming in the company of their enemies, he thought, he would never get the chance to talk to them. He would talk to the *Chalaques* for the Senikas, and if the *Chalaques* agreed, then he would arrange a meeting between the two peoples somewhere. That would be the best way.

Young Puppy found himself in the land of the *Ofos*, and he knew that he would have to be watchful. He was not afraid of them, but they were not his prey. They were merely a nuisance to him, and he didn't want to allow anyone to catch him by surprise and interfere with his plans.

The trail he rode was well traveled, and he came to a place where it was wide and straight for a long way ahead. To the right the land was flat, though it was dotted with boulders and clumps of trees. To the left a green and rocky hillside rose sharply.

Then up ahead he saw them. *Ofos* almost for sure. There were twelve at least, and they were armed with bows and arrows. His earlier fantasy of riding hard and fast into a group of warriors flashed through his mind again, and he saw it then as completely foolish.

He was probably, he thought, just out of range of a good bow shot, but if he started to ride toward them, before he could get near enough to be a real threat, they would loose their arrows, likely shooting him right out of the saddle. Charging them would only give them a good target.

He knew that he could easily outdistance them on his *sogwili*, but if he did that, there was only one way to go, and that was back where he had come from. He did not want to turn around and run. He decided to sit still there in the road and wait for them to make the first move.

For a time it seemed as if the *Ofos* had decided the same. They stood there in a bunch looking at him and talking to one another. Several of them had fitted arrows to their bows, but they had not lifted them up or pulled them back. They just watched him, as he was watching them.

He looked around, and he saw to his right a stand of trees where he could leave his horse. To his left and up ahead, a short climb up the steep hillside, was a clump of boulders. The largest of the bunch was almost as high, he estimated, as his shoulders. He decided that he would get his horse behind the trees to his right and climb behind the high boulders to his left.

Then one of the *Ofos* stepped forward and screamed, and the screams of the others joined his in a weird cacophony of threatening sound. They came running toward him, hard and fast. He rode to the trees and left his horse behind them. On foot, his own bow and quiver of arrows in his hands, he ran for the rocks. Just as he started to climb, the *Ofos* stopped and released their arrows. As he dropped behind the boulders, arrows struck the ground around him. A few bounced off the rocks he crouched behind.

He nocked an arrow and stood up, aiming and releasing fast. His arrow hit its mark. An *Ofo* fell. He ducked again, and arrows rained around him. Again he stood and let one fly. This time his arrow struck an *Ofo* in the shoulder. Just before he dropped again behind his boulder, Young Puppy saw a man help the wounded one back a safe distance. That last shot of his had been better than a killing. It had taken two out of the fight.

More arrows fell around him, and he raised up again to shoot, but the *Ofos* had also taken cover. He dropped again, peering around the edge of the boulder, looking for a target. Then an *Ofo* warrior screamed and came running toward him, war club raised.

Young Puppy stood and aimed, but as he did, so did another *Ofo*, and the *Ofo* let fly first. Young Puppy leaned to his right as he released his own arrow, and he felt the *Ofo* missile tear through his left ear. His own arrow sank into the chest of the charging man, who fell onto his back just at the foot of the hill.

Young Puppy ducked again, and he could feel the warm, sticky blood from his ear running down his neck and onto his shoulder. So, he thought, they have a new tactic to use against me. One charges, and when I rise up to shoot, another one is waiting to shoot at me. He eased himself over to one side of the boulder and peeked around. There were still eight men out there somewhere. He thought that he would probably be killed that day, and then he recalled the strange prophecy of the old woman, Uyona, and he wondered when and where he would be reborn and what he would be like.

Then he saw a man stand up cautiously, his bow held ready. If they tried the same trick on him again, there would be another rush coming. This time, he thought, I'll be ready for them. I'll aim for the bowman first. They can't pull the same trick on me twice. He pulled his war club loose from where it dangled at his waist and laid it near at hand. He nocked an arrow. He waited.

He heard a shriek. He did not stand. He leaned around the boulder's edge, pulled back the string and released the arrow. It drove itself into the pit of the startled bowman's stomach, and the *Ofo* arrow went skiddering in the dust of the road, but this time two men had charged, and they were almost up to the boulders where Young Puppy waited.

He tossed aside his bow, grabbed his war club and swung it at the first to arrive, crashing it into the side of the man's head. The *Ofo* fell back against his own companion, causing that one to lose his balance on the steep hillside. Then Young Puppy heard the sound of loose rocks falling behind him on the hillside. Someone was coming down at his back from up above. The man below had scrambled to his feet and was coming back up toward Young Puppy. At the same time Young Puppy saw the rest of the *Ofos* down below rise up from their hiding places at once and rush toward him. They were coming at him from both sides. This was it, he thought. Here he would die.

He whirled and swung his club, and he felt it smash a skull. He saw the body drop at his feet, and he knew that something was wrong, but he didn't have time to worry about it just then. He turned to face the onslaught. He was ready to die, but he would die fighting like a Real Person. He braced himself. For once he was glad of Uyona's crazy prophecy. It gave him a strange kind of comfort, a sense of immortality.

Suddenly there was a sound like thunder and then an-

other and a third. The charging *Ofos* stopped and turned to
look back down the road. Young Puppy looked too. The
horseback company of Jacques Tournier was charging fast
and firing their guns. The *Ofos*, frightened and confused,
turned and fled.

Young Puppy stood there beside the boulders and waited
until Tournier had come to a halt just beneath him in the
road. The Catawba, Little Black Bear, rode up beside him.
The two of them looked up and, recognizing Young
Puppy, smiled.

"Young Puppy, *mon ami*," said Tournier, "I'm glad we
came upon you when we did."

Little Black Bear translated for him, and Young Puppy
made his response.

"*Wado*," he said. "I thought that I was going to die today
right here. Probably I would have, too, had you not come
along."

Tournier could see that Young Puppy was covered with
blood.

"You're hurt, *mon ami*," he said. "Come on down and let
us tend to your wound."

"It's only my ear," said Young Puppy. "It's not bad. Ears
just bleed a lot."

He looked back at the body lying at his feet, the body of
the man who had come at him from behind. It was lying
there facedown, but it did not have the look of an *Ofo*. It
had another look, a look familiar to Young Puppy. He tried
to tell himself he must be wrong. He did not want to think
it. He knelt beside the body, and he touched it. He hesitated. Then he turned it over.

An anguished wail escaped the mouth of Young Puppy,

and it startled Tournier and his entire company. Tournier dismounted quickly and ran up the hill to stop by the side of Young Puppy, whose wail by then had turned to sobs. The Frenchman looked down and saw the body of his first *Chalaque* friend, the one they called Asquan'.

Twenty

TOURNIER had all his men dismount. He ordered some to drag away the bodies of the fallen *Ofo* warriors and others to set up a temporary camp for rest. He could tell that Young Puppy was not going to be ready to travel any time soon, and he did not want to leave the young man alone in the state he was in. He told his men to be quiet and respectful, and then he settled down to wait. Sitting still and unoccupied, he noticed that there was a slight chill in the air. The summer would be over soon in this land, he thought.

At last Young Puppy's wailing and sobbing ceased, but he did not move. He sat in silence beside the body of Asquani, his friend whom he had killed. Still Tournier waited a respectable time before, bringing along Little Black Bear, he approached Young Puppy.

"*Mon ami*," he said, speaking through the interpreter. "Asquani was my friend too. We two fought the Spanish together. His is a great loss to us all. With you, we weep for him. But he died fighting bravely by your side against these *Ofo*. It is an honorable death for a soldier to die in battle."

When Young Puppy heard the translation of Tournier's words, he looked up at the Frenchman with a terrible thought. Puzzled, Tournier looked over at Little Black Bear for help.

"Did I say something wrong?" he asked.

Little Black Bear could only shrug. Ah well, the Frenchman thought, he feels the loss deeply. There is nothing quite so devastating for a soldier as the loss of a close comrade in arms. And these two men were close friends and companion soldiers.

"We will help you give your friend a proper burial," said Tournier. "There's nothing more to do now. I'm very sorry, *mon ami*. Ah well, I'll have some men prepare a grave."

"No," said Young Puppy. "Not here. I must take him home."

Tournier considered both the inconvenience and the unpleasantness of such a chore, but he shrugged away the thought. He hesitated only a moment.

"*Eh bien,*" he said. "Then we will accompany you back to your home."

They wrapped the body carefully, then constructed a travois upon which to transport it back to the land of the Real People. Young Puppy, along with Tournier's entire company, mounted up. Slowly they started riding south.

They did not cover much distance the rest of that day, and when the sun was low in the western sky, they stopped and made a camp for the night. Young Puppy refused the food they offered him.

He sat alone at the edge of the camp. The side of his head was throbbing from the tear in his left ear. He had refused to allow Docteur DuBois to treat it. The wound had not even been washed. He thought about Uyona and her prediction, and he wondered if she had somehow got it wrong.

He was alive, and Asquani was dead. Perhaps she had misinterpreted something. She had seen the wrong man dead. Or maybe her prediction had been valid, but somehow Young Puppy had perverted it, and caused the death that had been meant for him to fall on his friend instead.

But no. He realized then that the old woman's prediction must come true, for when the news reached home, Young Puppy would have to die. It was the law. A life must pay for a life. Things must always balance out. A profound sadness settled into the soul of Young Puppy.

Such a short time ago he had been full of joy and hope, and then had come the hateful words of old Uyona. Now Asquani was dead, and now Young Puppy would have to die. The life he had imagined for himself with Guwisti would never be. He felt guilty for grieving over his own future, for thinking of the beauty and charms of Guwisti, with the body of Asquani, so recently killed, lying so near.

Then he recalled the rest of the old woman's prediction, that he would die and be reborn, that he and Guwisti would marry in a year. How could that happen now? He didn't want to think about it. It held out a strange and slender kind of hope, and he told himself that there was none.

Tournier came to him again, bringing along Little Black Bear. The Frenchman sat down beside Young Puppy. For a moment he kept his silence.

"*Mon ami*," he said at last, "times like this are bad, and I know it seems just now that it will always be so. But believe me, it will get better. Time heals all wounds. You'll see."

Young Puppy shook his head. He did not look at Tournier or at Little Black Bear. He stared blankly at the ground before him.

"I have very little time," he said. "I'm going home to die."

When Tournier heard Young Puppy's words translated, his face registered surprise, almost shock.

"What can he mean?" he asked Little Black Bear. "Ask him what he means by that. He's young and strong. He has no wounds. He should have many years of life ahead of him. Ask him what he means."

Young Puppy listened to the question, and only then did he realize that the Frenchman was ignorant of what had really happened to Asquani. Of course he couldn't know. Young Puppy had been too distracted before to think about anything other than his own grief. For the first time, he looked up into the face of Jacques Tournier.

"I killed my friend," he said. "Not the *Ofos*. For that I have to die."

Young Puppy did not want to talk more about the killing of Asquani, and in response to Tournier's further questions, he gave short answers. Eventually, Tournier had the story pieced together. Somehow, he decided, Asquani had come upon the fight between Young Puppy and the *Ofos*, and he had gotten himself up above the hillside. He had come down to join his friend in battle, but he had come too fast. Perhaps he had slipped on loose rocks and come down more quickly than he intended.

At any rate, Young Puppy, under attack from the front and in the heat of battle, heard the noise behind him and reacted to it. He turned and killed his friend before he realized who was there. He thought an *Ofo* had somehow gotten behind him.

"Don't blame yourself, *mon ami*," he said. "*Un accident.* It's unfortunate. Terrible. But these things happen. We go on."

Little Black Bear stood silent.

"Well?" said Tournier. "Tell him what I said."

"You don't understand," said the interpreter. "The ways of his people, the *Chalaques*, make no distinction between an accident and purposeful killing. When a *Chalaque* kills one of his own, then he or another member of his clan must die. Someone from the clan of the dead man will kill Young Puppy to balance things between the two clans. That's their way."

"Ah," said Tournier, "is there no escape for him?"

Little Black Bear gave a shrug.

"Sometimes a payment can be made by the killer to the dead man's clan," he said, "but in this case, I don't know. The head was clearly crushed by Young Puppy's war club. Sometimes another member of the killer's clan can die in his place, but even if someone is willing, I don't think this one would allow it. No. I think your *Chalaque* friend will die."

It was cool and overcast when they reached the land of the Real People, and Tournier was hoping now for several reasons that the *Chalaques* would allow him to go into one of their towns. He had the Senika peace proposal to present. He hoped to plead Young Puppy's case, and he did not want to get caught out in the open if a storm came through. Besides, his horses needed rest and grass.

At the pass outside Kituwah, the Wolves stopped them on the road. Trotting Wolf was there, and he remembered Jacques Tournier from the fight at the Dark Island against the *Ani-Asquani*. He spoke briefly to Young Puppy, welcoming him home, and then he turned to Tournier.

The Frenchman told Trotting Wolf, through Little Black Bear, that he was aware of the *Chalaques'* rule to keep all foreigners out of their land. He understood their reasons, but he hoped that they would reconsider this one time. He was, of course, still interested in trade, but more important, he said, he had come from the Senikas with a plea for peace.

Finally, he said, he had come upon Young Puppy and Asquani in a fight against the *Ofos*. Asquani had been killed. Tournier modestly told Trotting Wolf that his men had driven off the *Ofos* and then determined to serve as escort for Young Puppy and the body on their journey home. He said nothing of the manner of Asquani's death. It was not the time, he thought, and he knew that it was not his place. Trotting Wolf listened to all that Tournier had to say, and then he told the Frenchmen to camp beside the road and wait, while he went into Kituwah to present their case.

They were friends, Trotting Wolf argued. They had helped the Real People in fights against their enemies more than once. They were not at all like the cruel *Ani-*

Asquani. In fact, those other whites were their sworn enemies too. They did not intend to establish permanent set-
tlements, and they were not looking for the yellow metal
that the Spaniards were so crazy for. They were interested
only in trade, and they had many fine goods which could
be of use to the Real People.

Besides, the old year was gone. The ceremony for the
New Year had just concluded, and storm clouds were
threatening in the sky. It would not be good, he said, to
send anyone away at such a time. The Real People had
rules of hospitality regarding travelers, and Trotting Wolf
argued that it would not be good .to violate those rules at
this particular time with these particular people.

"It would be a mistake," he said, "for us to think all
white men are alike. If they thought of us in that same way,
then they would think that we and the *Ani-Gusa* and the
Ani-Senika and others are all the same."

Then he told them of the special mission that the
Frenchmen had come on. They had come from the *Ani-
Senika* with an offer of peace. At this point some angry
voices rose up in protest.

"How could these white men be our friends if they are
friends with our enemies?"

Some did not want peace with the Senikas. Some did.
Trotting Wolf waited until the angry voices died down.

"I'm not here to talk about the Senikas," he said. "We
shouldn't argue over that now. We should let the white
men in and listen to what they have to say. Then we can
argue about the Senikas."

At last he told them of Asquani's death and how the
Frenchmen had saved Young Puppy from the *Ofos*

and brought him back home, along with the body of As-quan'.

"Let them come in," he said, and no more voices were raised in opposition. And so the first exception was made to the long-standing rule regarding outsiders, and Trotting Wolf returned to the Frenchmen's camp with the news.

Twenty-one

THEY RODE to Kituwah and, leaving their horses outside the wall, walked into the town, where they were welcomed warmly. Many of the residents of Kituwah had never seen a white man, and they flocked around the Frenchmen with curiosity. Guwisti was thrilled to see Young Puppy safely back from wherever he had gone, but she was greatly puzzled by his reticence.

"What's wrong?" she asked him.

"It's nothing to do with my feeling for you," he said, "but my life is over. There can be nothing more between us."

Guwisti backed slowly away from him. Then she turned and ran to find her mother. Young Puppy walked over to Trotting Wolf.

"I have a tale to tell," he said. "It's about the death of Asquani."

Word went out all over town that there would be a meeting that night in the townhouse, and everyone was excited. The festive mood from the recent ceremony was still in the air. Now they would all gather to hear from the strange white men, and to hear the battle stories of Young Puppy. All the excitement, though, was tempered by the news of Asquani's death. It was as if a pleasant day was overcast by clouds.

At the house of Osa no rays of sun broke through the clouds. Her world was black. Asquani was dead. She mourned. She wailed. She cut her hair. And when she had no more tears and no more energy with which to cry, she sat in her dark and lonely house. She longed to join Asquani in death, and she likely would have done so. But she was carrying his child. She knew she would have to live for the child. But she also knew there would be no other meaning in her life.

Young Puppy begged Trotting Wolf to allow him to speak first at the meeting.

"I'll be brief," he said. "Then I'll be out of the way, and the important business of the council can proceed."

Strange words, thought Trotting Wolf, but he agreed.

Diguhsgi tried to comfort her daughter. They sat inside the house, Guwisti's head upon her mother's breast, her mother's arms around her.

"He was cold to me, Mother," she said. "He was not even like himself. I don't know what's wrong."

Diguhsgi felt her daughter's tears soak through her dress. She held her close and rocked.

"I don't know," she said, "but remember the words of old Horn. He'll have to die, and then he'll be reborn, and it will take a year. Be patient. Try to be strong and brave. Maybe all will be well yet."

The townhouse that night was full. It seemed to Jacques Tournier that not another soul could get inside, and then he thought, why would one want to? He was anxious to get the ordeal over with and done himself. The bench seats were not comfortable to sit on for a long period of time, and the air was full of smoke, smoke from the central fire and tobacco smoke from the many pipes that various people puffed. He breathed the smoke, and it burned his eyes.

Following some preliminary words by Trotting Wolf, Young Puppy stood to speak. The crowded room had grown so quiet that Tournier thought he could hear the crackle of the burning tobacco in the nearest pipes.

"I was fighting the *Ofos*," said Young Puppy, "when Asquani came to help me. He came up behind me. I didn't know who was there. I turned quickly, and I struck out with my war club, not seeing who it was. I, not the *Ofos*, killed Asquani, and now I am ready to die."

There were murmurs from the crowd.

"Asquani was a Wolf Person," Young Puppy continued. "You Wolves can kill me now."

Trotting Wolf gave a glance to some of his brother Wolves. One opened his mouth as if to speak, but Trotting Wolf made a gesture to silence the man. Their brows all wrinkled. No one spoke. No one made a move toward Young Puppy.

"I'm going to Stikoyi to see my mother one last time," said Young Puppy, "unless you kill me on the way. If you catch me on the road before I get there, I won't resist. I won't defend myself. If I make it to Stikoyi, I'll stay there. I won't run away. You can find me there."

He turned and walked to the door and on outside. The large crowd in the townhouse was silent. Then Diguhsgi touched her daughter and spoke to her in a desperate whisper.

"Stop him," she said.

"What? Why?"

"You know Kituwah is the Peace Town. No one can harm him here."

Guwisti's face lit up with hope, and she ran to catch Young Puppy. Trotting Wolf made a quick motion, and two Wolves got up and followed her outside. Young Puppy was almost to the place where the two ends of the fence around the town overlapped to make the way in or out. He stepped into the passageway. Guwisti ran hard. She reached out and grabbed him by the shoulder. He stopped and turned to look at her. The two Wolves stopped some steps behind. They stood watching and waiting, saying nothing.

"Wait," said Guwisti. "Don't go."

He looked into her eyes with deep longing and sadness. He wanted to take her in his arms and hold her close. Instead he shook his head.

"It's no use," he said. "You heard me tell what happened."

"Young Puppy," she said, "listen to me. Have you forgotten that Kituwah is the Peace Town? No one can kill you here. No one can touch you unless you step outside these walls."

Of course he knew about Kituwah. All Real People knew about the Peace Town. But in his misery, he had not thought about it. He saw her face pleading with him, reflecting hope and joy, and he felt the love that had meant everything to him not long ago. He wanted to listen to her. He wanted to stay.

"But Asquani was my friend," he said, "and I killed him. Would it not be cowardly of me to stay inside these walls?"

"How can it be cowardly?" said Guwisti. "The Peace Town exists for just that purpose. Do you think that 'Squani would want you to die? Stay here for me."

"The New Year has just begun," said Young Puppy. "I'd have to stay inside this town for an entire year."

"Yes," said Guwisti, and she smiled a knowing smile. "For a full year."

"All right," he said. "I'll stay for at least a while and think about it."

From a shadow by the wall a short distance away, the shining eyes of Uyona, the Horn, watched as Guwisti took Young Puppy by the arm and led him back into the town. The two Wolves looked at each other, then turned and headed back for the townhouse. Uyona smiled.

It was late the next afternoon at a reconvened meeting before the business of the Frenchmen was concluded by the council. Tournier received instructions to go back to the Senikas with the message that the Real People were willing to meet with them and talk of peace. But Trotting Wolf also told him that there was no hurry. Tournier and his company were welcome to wait out the stormy weather and rest and fatten up their *sogwilis* in Kituwah. There would be time enough to return to the Senikas.

The people of Kituwah also agreed to trade with Tournier, but they stopped short of forming an alliance with the King of France. Though Tournier, they said, would always be welcome.

In response to the Frenchman's curiosity regarding the status of Young Puppy, Trotting Wolf explained to him the special role of Kituwah among the Real People.

"Kituwah is a Mother Town," he said, "one of our oldest towns. From it sprang many other towns. And Kituwah is the Peace Town. It is forbidden for anyone to kill inside its walls. We Wolves are obliged by our clan law to kill Young Puppy because of what happened to Asquani, but we cannot do it here. If he should leave Kituwah, we will kill him."

"You mean," said Tournier, incredulous, "that he must stay inside this town forever in order to avoid being killed?"

"What?" said Trotting Wolf. "Oh no. At the beginning of each New Year, everything begins again. Everything of the past is forgotten."

"But you have just had your ceremony for the New Year," said Tournier.

"Yes."

"So in order to live, Young Puppy must remain in this town for a full year?"

"Yes."

"Then he will be forgiven?"

"Yes," said Trotting Wolf. "If he can stay inside these walls for all that time."

Glossary

Cherokee words, phrases, and names used in *The War Trail North*

Alesta   female private parts.

Ani-Asquani   Spanish People (*ani*, plural prefix + *Asquani*, a Spaniard). See *Asquani* below.

Ani-Chahta   Choctaw People.

Ani-Chiksa   Chickasaw People.

Ani-Gusa   Muskogee or Creek People. Also spelled *Cusa* or *Coosa*.

Ani-Kutani   an ancient Cherokee priesthood, overthrown by the people when they became too tyrannical (*ani*, plural prefix + *Kutani*, a priest).

Ani-Quanuhgi   Delaware People.

Ani-Sawahoni   Shawnee People.

Ani-Senika   Seneca People.

Ani-Tsisqua   Bird People, or the Bird Clan, one of the seven Cherokee clans.

Ani-wahya   Wolf People, or the Wolf Clan, one of seven Cherokee clans (*ani* + *wahya*, wolf).

Ani-yunwi-ya   the Real People (*ani* + *yunwi*, person + *ya*, real or original).

Aquanuhgi   a Delaware Person.

Asquani   a Spaniard, "Cherokeeized" version of the Spanish word *Español.*

Awi   deer.

Awi-ekwa   elk, or big deer. Literally, deer big.

Awi-usdi   little deer, the name of the spirit chief of all the deer.

Ayuh   I, personal pronoun.

Ayuh Awi-ekwa   I am Elk (or Big Deer).

Diguhsgi   spider. In *The War Trail North*, a woman's name. The spider is a weaver, and, in Cherokee mythology, the spider is also the bringer of fire.

Elikwa   enough, or "That's enough."

Etsi   Mother.

Gahawista   pounded dried corn.

Gatayusti   an ancient Cherokee gambling game, played with a stone disc and a spear.

Gayahulo   a saddle.

Gayule jiwonuh   I will speak no more.

Golanuh   raven.

Golanuh Ahyelisgi   raven mocker, one who steals the remaining life from another to add to his own.

Gusa-dihi   Creek killer. A masculine name.

Guwist'   contracted form of *Guwisti* (see below).

Guwisti   sifter or sieve, made like a basket but with a looser weave. Also a woman's name.

Hla gohusdi   nothing *(hla,* negative prefix + *gohusdi,* something).

Howa   all right, or okay.

Jisdu   rabbit, also spelled *tsisdu,* or *chisdu.*

Kanohena   a thick drink or soup made from hominy, traditionally served to guests.

Kanona   a stump of a tree, the top of which has been

scooped out to form a bowl. It's used as a pounding stump.

Kituwah also spelled Keetoowah. The name of an ancient Cherokee town, thought to have been the Mother Town of the Real People, also a Peace or Sanctuary Town. It is also currently the name of an old full-blood Cherokee religious and nationalistic organization, the Keetoowah Society, and of a federally recognized tribal government for the Cherokees, the United Keetoowah Band of Cherokees in Oklahoma.

Kutani a priest. See *Ani-Kutani* above.

Lolo a locust or cicada. In *The War Trail North*, a woman's name.

Nihina and you?

Nuhdadewi big trading month (November).

Olig' contracted form of *Oliga* (see below).

Oliga the redhorse fish. In *The War Trail North*, a masculine name.

Osd' contracted form of *osda*, good or well.

Osiyo a greeting.

'Siyo contracted form of *osiyo*, a greeting.

Sogwil' contracted form of *sogwili* (see below).

Sogwili a horse. Literally, he carries it on his back.

'Squani contracted form of *Asquani*, Spaniard.

Stikoyi an old town name.

Tohigwu I am well. Response to *Tohiju?* (see below).

Tohiju how are you?

Uduji uncle.

Uh or *uh-uh* yes.

Uk'ten' contraction of *ukitena*, a legendary monster from Cherokee tales. He is like a giant rattlesnake with wings and antlers. He breathes fire, and his very look can kill.

Ulunsuti   a divining crystal said to come from the forehead of the *ukitena*. See *uk'ten'* above. Literally, transparent.

Usdi   little or small, also "little one" or baby.

Uyona   horn.

Wado   thank you.

Watoli   the male sex organ.

Yansa   buffalo, or, more correctly, the American bison.

Yona-hawiya   bear meat.

Words and phrases used in *The War Trail North* other than Cherokee or English

Catawba   a southeastern American Indian tribe.

Chalakee   Choctaw and possibly Mobilian trade language, or jargon, word for the Cherokees. Likely the source of the word "Cherokee."

Chalaque   early French for "Cherokee" (from *Chalakee*, above).

Gana   (Seneca word) a masculine name.

Ga-ne-ah-go-oh-noh   Seneca word for the Mohawks, People of the Flint.

Hiadeoni   (Seneca word) a masculine name.

Nun-da-wa-oh-noh   (Seneca word) People of the Great Hill, the Seneca People.

Ofo   an American Indian tribe from the Ohio Valley, short for *Ofogoula* (Dog People), from the trade language. They were also known as *Mosopelea*.

Ong-weh-oh-weh   (Seneca word) People of the Extended Lodge, the Iroquois League, also known as the League of Five Nations (later Six Nations), consisting of the

Mohawk, Seneca, Cayuga, Onondaga, Oneida, and later the Tuscarora People.

Oyada'ge'onnon (Seneca word) Cave People, the Seneca designation for the Cherokee People.

Timucua an American Indian tribe native to Florida.

ABOUT THE AUTHOR

Robert J. Conley is one of the most respected Native American writers at work today. He is a two-time winner of the prestigious Spur Award from the Western Writers of America for his short story "Yellow Bird," and for his 1992 novel *Nickajack*. *The War Trail North* is the seventh novel in a series about Conley's own Cherokee heritage. He lives in Tahlequah, Oklahoma.

ABOUT THE ILLUSTRATOR

Painter/pipemaker Murv Jacob, a descendant of the Kentucky Cherokees, lives and works in Tahlequah, Oklahoma. His meticulously researched, brightly colored, intricate work centers on the traditional Southeastern Indian cultures and has won numerous awards.